MM 672
a B

DESDEMONA

DEATH COMES FOR DESDEMONA

NINA COOMBS PYKARE

THORNDIKE
CHIVERS

LF/3648546

This Large Print edition is published by Thorndike Press, Waterville, Maine USA and by BBC Audiobooks Ltd, Bath, England.
Thorndike Press is an imprint of Thomson Gale, a part of the Thomson Corporation.
Thorndike is a trademark and used herein under license.

LIBRARY OF CONGRESS CATALOGING-IN-PUBLICATION DATA

Pykare, Nina.
   Death comes for Desdemona / by Nina Coombs Pykare.
     p. cm. — (Thorndike Press large print candlelight)
   ISBN 0-7862-8940-6 (alk. paper)
     1. Actresses — Fiction. 2. London (England) — Fiction. 3. Large type books. I. Title.
   PS3566.Y48D42 2006
   813'.54—dc22   2006019961

BRITISH LIBRARY CATALOGUING-IN-PUBLICATION DATA AVAILABLE

Published in 2006 in the U.S. by arrangement with
Maureen Moran Agency.
Published in 2007 in the U.K. by arrangement with the author.

U.K. Hardcover: 978 1 405 63942 2 (Chivers Large Print)
U.K. Softcover: 978 1 405 63943 9 (Camden Large Print)

Printed in the United States of America on permanent paper.
10 9 8 7 6 5 4 3 2 1

DEATH COMES FOR DESDEMONA

CHAPTER ONE

If Papa hadn't insisted on coming to London that April, none of this would have happened. I wouldn't have met Archie and we wouldn't have found the dead — but I'm getting ahead of myself.

We came to London because Papa had made plans for us and we knew better than to argue with him. Papa was the head of our family and of our troupe of strolling players. Charles Ketterling, "The Great Tragedian," he billed himself, though much as I loved him, I knew he wasn't great; just a run-of-the-mill actor, somewhat the worse for too much gin. Papa was partial to gin — so much so that in theater circles he was known as "Blue Ruin Ketterling."

Mama, Esther Smithfield Ketterling, never touched a drop of liquor. Mama was the real center of our family, although big blustery Papa made a lot of noise. Small quiet Mama made things happen. Mama was not a great actress either, but she did well enough for our little troupe. And she kept the rest of us going.

Then there was me, Catherine Louise Ketterling, Kate — sort of a mixture of the two of them — brash, cheeky, sassy, impertinent. Papa called me all those and more. And he was right. My line of business on the stage was the hoyden and I was good at it, maybe because that was closest to the real me.

Anyway, when several important members of our traveling troupe left us early that spring, we were forced to disband. Papa wrote to Mr. Kemble because the two of them had once been strolling players together. Since then Mr. Kemble had come up in the world, not only acting, but managing Covent Garden Theater, and he agreed to give us employment. Papa told him that I could make people laugh and that in a breeches part I could draw a full house. Mr. Kemble might believe that's all Papa had in mind, but I knew better. I knew that Papa, strange as it seemed, meant to make me the greatest tragic actress London had ever seen.

"Motive," Papa always said. "Look for what's behind a character's actions. Know that and you know her." And so I was always wondering about a person's reason, his *why*.

Take Papa now. Papa said the Blue Ruin was the reason he wasn't rivaling Mr. Kemble as London's greatest tragic actor. "I got me a fondness for gin," he would say sadly to anyone who would listen. "Otherwise I'd be there in London, putting the great Kemble to shame."

Mama and I kept our tongues between our teeth, but we knew better. Though we never mentioned it to each other, we knew that Papa was a mediocre actor and that his partiality for gin was not the cause of his mediocrity, but the effect of it.

Anyway, we were in London and I had good acting work. Mama sewed costumes and Papa hung around the theater, interfering wherever he could, and probably driving poor Mr. Kemble mad.

I was pleased to get to see the great Sarah Siddons play Lady Macbeth. I knew why Papa wanted me to play tragic parts. The biggest rewards, the most fame, went to those who did tragedy. But I also knew that tragedy was not for me. And no amount of watching another actress, or studying her dramatic ways, would change that.

We hadn't seen much of the city except right around the theater, and there it was dirty, infested with pick pockets and beggars and worse, but we were real pleased with the theater, a fancy place, all gilt and velvet, much better than the barns and inns we played in the provinces.

I performed well and Mr. Kemble told Papa he was pleased. Then one day, a little more than two weeks after our arrival, Mr. Kemble announced that Mrs. Siddons would be unable to perform as Desdemona in Othello. She had taken ill and Nell Stanford would take over the part instead. Papa glowered at hearing of Nell's good fortune, but I could only be glad the part hadn't fallen to me. Even with a dark wig hiding my red curls and heavy make up on my freckled face, I couldn't begin to look suitably tragic.

No one in the company much liked Nell. She had good looks and the long dark hair and voluptuous figure that many men seem to favor. Her looks were great, even I said that, though not without a little envy. But her character was something else. During rehearsal she was often downright nasty to the other actors, and she treated her dresser Betty like dirt.

My dressing room was next to Nell's, and that afternoon, after she found she was to play Desdemona, I heard a terrible commotion next door, screaming and cursing and things crashing against the wall. Then poor Betty rushed out with a big cut on her forehead.

I took Betty into my room and cleaned the cut. Her eyes rolled and she hiccuped, holding back her sobs.

"Does it hurt much?" I asked anxiously.

She shook her head. "No, miss. 'Tain't that. It's the mistress. She'll be that angered with me fer running out."

"Nonsense," I declared, my opinion of Nell sinking even lower. "She can't expect you to stand there while she throws things at you."

Betty looked surprised, her round face screwed up in a puzzled frown. "But she do, miss. And I don't want to lose me place. I got a mother in Fleet Street what needs me and I'm the only one as can —"

"If Nell dismisses you," I said indignantly, "you come right to me. *I'll* hire you."

I shouldn't have said such a thing, of course. I had very little in the way of funds of my own. Even though I was nineteen, Papa, as head of the family, collected my wages and gave me what he thought I needed. Mama always said I had this bad habit of acting on impulse first and regretting it later. But I knew I could talk Papa into hiring Betty if I had to.

"That's most kind of you, miss," Betty said gratefully. "If I could only find that paper she's a-worrying over. She's always putting things away and then blaming me if I can't find 'em."

That sounded like Nell, all right. Even in the short time I'd been there I'd seen how she thought. Anything that went wrong was always someone else's fault, never Nell's.

I had Betty's cut cleaned and the flow of blood stopped. "You'll find it, I'm sure," I said, patting her arm. "Just remember, I'm here and I'm your friend."

"Thank 'ee, miss. Yer most kind," and she hurried out.

I had no role in Othello, but I often stood in the wings to watch Mrs. Siddons at work. One night I went out to watch Nell Stanford. Of course, Othello had the best part. Mr. Kemble was in fine fettle as the Moor, declaiming in that rich deep voice of his. I thought his gestures a little over dramatic, but I knew Papa would approve.

Nell's Desdemona, though, was definitely watery. I'd never cared much for the part of Desdemona. It didn't help me to try to understand her either — to try to imagine what was behind her actions. I certainly wouldn't submit meekly to being smothered and then before I died try to absolve the scoundrel who did it! It's a man's world, of course, and I knew it, but I didn't have to like it.

The part of Emilia, Desdemona's friend and lady in waiting, was more to my liking. She wasn't afraid to stand up to Othello. But I wouldn't be playing her either. Lavinia Patrick, the company's female heavy, had dibs on it.

I liked Lavinia. She had the looks to play the villainess, but in spite of her large body and fierce visage, she had the tenderest of hearts. I'd seen her several times giving coins to the young boys who called the actors to the stage. When I joined the company, Lavinia had been the one to welcome me, to show me around the theater, while the spiteful Nell pretended I didn't exist.

A hand descending on my shoulder made me jump. "Evening there, Kate."

I eased out from under Peter Rutherford's large sweaty hand. "Evening, Peter." Peter had already tried to make a liaison with me and been quite definitely refused. He couldn't seem to take no for an answer. "No" was all he'd get from me, however, because he was also rude, and far too free with his hands for the taste of any virtuous, or even discriminating, woman.

When the play was over, those of us not in the afterpiece were standing around in the greenroom discussing the performance when suddenly screams rang out. There was a mad scramble to get out the door and everyone hurried off toward the sound.

Nell Stanford came careening down the hall, screaming and blubbering, her face six different shades of red. Papa tried to get her to stop long enough to tell him what was wrong, but she didn't make a bit of sense. She just kept pointing back down the hall toward her dressing room and blubbering. I left Papa and the others clustered around her and followed Mr. Kemble down the hall.

I got to Nell's door just behind him. "My God!" he exclaimed, crossing the room and dropping to one knee.

The crumpled form on the floor was wearing the cloak Nell used in the first act as Desdemona, but I could see the cut on her forehead. Betty. My stomach jumped up into my mouth and my knees quit holding me up.

I sank down beside Mr. Kemble. "Is she —"

"She's dead," he said, his great voice sadly muted. "Strangled." He touched the cloak. "Who could have done such a thing?"

My first thought was Nell Stanford, but

much as I disliked the hot-tempered Nell, I couldn't see her strangling anyone. She was more apt to hit them over the head with the nearest object. Besides, why would she wreck her own dressing room? The place was in chaos — torn playbills and rumpled costumes scattered everywhere. Powder had been spilled on the dressing table and a bottle of cheap perfume lay on its side leaking a heavy sickening fragrance.

"We'll have to send for the Bow Street Runners," Mr. Kemble said, frowning. "Poor creature." He turned to me. "Find something to cover her with, will you, Kate?" And out he went, leaving me with the dead body.

I got to my feet, somewhat shaky but standing up at least, and looked around. A pink cashmere shawl lay in a heap under the clothes pegs and I spread it carefully over poor Betty. Now what would happen to the mother she'd been so worried about?

Then, my legs still shaky, I made my way to the door and leaned heavily against the frame. Death was no stranger to any of us, but to die like that, so brutally.

. . . and who would want to kill a poor dresser like Betty, a girl with nothing to steal, nothing to —

"I say, you look a bit pale. May I be of assistance?"

The speaker was a slight young man, elegantly dressed in the usual evening black. His fair hair wanted to stick up in all directions but his gray eyes regarded me warmly.

"I —" I tried to think. "There's been a murder and —"

"How awful for you," he said amiably. "Must make the knees a bit wobbly. Here, take my arm."

I stared at him, not moving. I wanted to be alone, perhaps to be sick to my stomach.

"Oh, yes," he said. "Forgot you don't know me. Name's Archie, Archibald Islington, Viscount Barrington, at your service."

I still didn't move.

"I was coming backstage to look for you," he said, unhooking my stiff fingers from the doorframe and pulling my arm through his, "and I heard the screaming."

My head was still whirling and my stomach still roiling, otherwise I wouldn't have accepted the support of his arm.

He smiled at me warmly. "I have wanted to make your acquaintance since I first saw you last week." He smiled, his pale little moustache lifting at one corner.

"I didn't intend to do it under such distressing circumstances, however." He

16

glanced into the room. "Poor thing. How dreadful."

I nodded. My strength was gradually coming back. I tried to ease my arm out of his, but his grasp was firm.

"Let me take you to the greenroom," he said, "where you can sit down."

And that's how I met Archie.

The Bow Street Runners assembled us all in the greenroom. Lavinia looked red-eyed, Nell sick, and Peter pale. The rest of the troupe didn't look much better, huddled together in their red velvet chairs, hardly able to take in what had happened.

I knew investigating crimes was just business to them, but I couldn't believe how indifferent, how hardened, the Bow Street Runners acted.

"A servant girl," Constable Kennedy said, as though that made Betty's murder less terrible. "Playin' at bein' her mistress. Probably kilt by some cracksman as thought he'd pick up a few pounds. Sneaked back here whilst the play was on." He turned to Nell who sat sniffling into a lace handkerchief. "Ye missin' anythin' valuable, miss?"

Nell shook her head. "It's hard to tell in such a mess but I don't think so. My jewels are all paste anyway."

The constable frowned. "Mayhap the thief didn't know that. It's robbery, I'm thinkin'. 'E didn't find nothin' and when the girl comes in on 'im, 'e panics and stops her mouth. 'E's well away now. Lotta people comes and go here. We'll likely never find 'im."

Next to me Archie snorted and quickly turned it into a cough, but he didn't fool me. He was as disgusted as I was with their callous attitude.

After a few more questions, the constable seemed satisfied and the Runners went off. Archie offered me his arm. "Allow me to escort you to your dressing room."

I was going to refuse, but just then Peter got up and started toward me. I didn't want him to go with me, and the prospect of going into my dressing room alone with Betty's poor body lying next door — and the murderer who knows where — didn't appeal to me, either. "Thank you," I said.

Archie looked all around my dressing room, even behind the changing screen and under the clothes on the pegs where no one could reasonably hope to go undetected. "No one here," he said cheerfully.

I realized later that cheerfulness was one of Archie's enduring — and endearing — qualities. It was part of the way he looked at life. And his cheerfulness was most welcome to me right then.

"Perhaps after you've changed, you'd care for a little supper," Archie said, running a hand through his already unruly hair.

"I —" Papa didn't approve of little suppers or the dalliances that often followed them. Papa had some rather rigid ideas about me saving myself for my art.

Archie moved a little closer. "You're very lovely," he said. "Prettiest thing I've ever seen."

I laughed. I couldn't help it. Imagine someone thinking I was that pretty — bright red hair, freckles, and slight of build. "All right," I said. "I'll go to supper with you but not because I believe that Banbury tale!"

Archie chuckled and put a hand dramatically on his waistcoat. "You have dealt me a mortal blow! A wound to the very heart!"

I went behind the screen to change my gown. "If I were you, milord —"

"Archie," he cried. "I insist. You must call me Archie!"

"Very well." I laughed again. "If I were you, Archie, I'd never try to make a career upon the stage. You're a dreadful actor."

"I know," he said, "but I played this part well. I made you feel better."

And to my surprise I realized he had.

CHAPTER TWO

Archie had his supper with me — and only his supper — and returned me to our rooms near the theater. Papa huffed about it a little, blowing out his cheeks and looking parental. But after all Archie was a peer. And even Papa thought peers a cut above ordinary people, so he didn't forbid me Archie's company. Not that I would have listened to him if he had, but still, it made things more pleasant.

It was the next morning before I thought again of Betty's poor mother, alone in that room off Fleet Street. I hadn't much to give her, but I would at least like to go to see her, to tell her I was sorry about Betty. I'd heard the tales of London's streets and what could happen to young women who ventured there alone, but I still wanted to go. I felt, somehow, that I owed it to Betty.

I thought of Archie who had, as he put it, plenty of pence in his pocket. Maybe when he came back to the theater again. . . . But since at our supper I had turned down his generous offer of "a pretty little establishment," and laughed while I did it, maybe he wouldn't come back. I tried to put those thoughts aside and concentrate on my lines as Polly in *The Beggar's Opera.* Still, I wished I had been a little kinder to Archie. He was a good enough sort and handsome in a boyish way, and he could have squired me about the city.

After a while I'd had enough of Polly and went to stand in the wings while Nell ran through her lines. I knew them all, of course. I had, in fact, played Desdemona myself out in the provinces. I'd cut my teeth on the great tragic parts — Desdemona, Juliet, Ophelia, Cordelia — even Lady Macbeth. I'd played them, though not particularly well.

Still, I was as good a Desdemona as Nell Stanford, probably better, though that didn't say much. Mrs. Siddons had a strong, sweet voice, Nell's was sharp, scratchy almost, and her Desdemona, rather than noble like Mrs. Siddons's, was whining and petulant.

I soon decided there was nothing to be learned by watching Nell at work. Besides, I wouldn't be playing Desdemona. Even if

Mrs. Siddons couldn't perform until after the arrival of her child, Nell would be waiting. And Nell wouldn't get sick, not with the chance to do the leading tragic roles.

I turned away in disgust and ran right into Archie's brocaded waistcoat. "Hold up there!" he said.

"Archie! How marvelous!" Smiling up at him, I grabbed his sleeve. "You're just the person I want to see."

"I am?" He raised an eyebrow in surprise. "Oh, Kate, dearest Kate, you've changed your mind about my offer! How wonderful!"

"No, Archie, not that." I patted his sleeve kindly.

He wrinkled his nose, it was sunburned I saw, and stammered out, "Sorry, I thought you wanted —" The red crept up his neck till it matched his nose.

Clutching his arm, I led him away from the stage. "I told you, Archie dear, I don't go in for keeping. Moreover, Papa would never allow it."

Even if it hadn't been against my principles, even if I'd decided to circumvent Papa and take a protector, I wouldn't have chosen Archie. He didn't make my heart stop in its tracks. He was older than me, but he seemed younger and boyish. Maybe because I had led such a varied life in the provinces, and Archie, as I found later, had only been on the town for a year.

I smiled at him. "But I would like a friend."

Archie's smile returned full force. "Here I am, then," he said cheerfully. "Your friend. What can I do for you?"

"I want to go to Fleet Street."

And Archie, bless him, just nodded, as though accompanying an actress he hardly knew to such a disreputable area was an everyday task. He didn't even ask me why I wanted to go there, he simply offered me his arm.

He helped me into the carriage and told the coachman, "Fleet Street."

I settled back on the squabs and smiled at him. I was really glad to see him, and not just because of Betty's mother, though I wouldn't tell *him* that. "Thank you, Archie. I do so want to see Betty's mother."

Fleet Street was even filthier than I'd imagined — crowded with all kinds of people, pickpockets, beggars, street sellers, none of whom looked much cleaner than the street whose cobblestones were slippery with rotting garbage and other filth I pre-ferred not to think about. Even the spring sunshine couldn't improve its looks. There was still a cold wind, a wind that carried the most horrible smells.

Looking a little pale, Archie helped me out of his carriage. "Kate, really, this place —"

"I know," I said, clutching his arm and pulling my cloak around me. In the provinces I'd seen some awful places, but nothing to compare to this.

Archie was a gem. He stood by me, somber-faced, while I asked about poor Betty's mother. We finally discovered someone who knew Mrs. Wattly. Her lodging was in an alley off the street, a room up a narrow flight of stairs so dark I could hardly see where to put my feet.

I rapped on the door twice, smartly, but there was no answer.

"Perhaps . . ." Archie began.

The door opened partway. The woman who stood there was slight and sickly looking. Her face was streaked with tears and she clutched a sodden gray rag of a handkerchief. Opening the door a little further, she stared at us with suspicion.

"I'm a friend of Betty's," I began. "From the theater. Kate —"

"Miss Kate!" She swung the door wide, her face transformed. "Oh, do come in."

24

The room was as gloomy as the stairs, cold and dank, with that chill that goes clear through and settles in the bones. There was no fire on the tiny hearth. What little light that filtered through the small dirty window showed a cot and a chair. A faint scrabbling in the walls indicated that Mrs. Wattly probably shared her home with rats. I pushed that out of my mind.

Mrs. Wattly pulled her tattered shawl closer around her and motioned to the single chair. "Do sit down, miss."

She looked from Archie to the cot but Archie said quickly, "I believe I'll stand."

Mrs. Wattly nodded, sinking wearily onto the side of the cot. "Betty told me as 'ow you was 'elpin' her. Betty was a good girl. She brung 'ome ever penny she made." She swallowed hastily and dabbed at her eyes.

"You wouldn't be knowin' if Mr. Kemble needs another seamstress, would you, miss? I used ta do sewin', till me fingers got so stiff." She straightened her frail shoulders. "I can do it again."

Behind me, Archie coughed. "Now, ain't that something," he said, dropping a warning hand on my shoulder. "And here's Kate just saying to me today that she's looking for someone handy with a needle."

The poor woman stared at me humbly.

25

"I'd be that proud, miss, if you'd give me a chance. With my Betty gone —"

She sobbed just once into the ragged handkerchief, then straightened. " 'Tis sorry, I am, miss. But my Betty, my Betty was a good girl. And those Bow Street Runners — they don't seem to care a bit who done it. There's only me and Willie who cares."

"Willie?" I asked. Did Betty have a brother?

"Aye. Wild Man Willie, they call him. He —"

"I've seen him," Archie said. "He's a pugilist, a good boxer."

"Aye. And 'e were that sweet on Betty. They was goin' ta marry and —" She swallowed again. "I can't see why no one would be wantin' ta kill my Betty. She wouldn't 'urt no one."

I nodded in sympathy. I had liked Betty. "She didn't have any enemies then?"

Mrs. Wattly frowned. "No, no enemies. But she was that worried 'bout somethin'. These last few days she was fidgety. And her and Willie was arguin' 'bout somethin'. She was a-feared, my Betty was."

"The constable thinks it was simple robbery," Archie said.

Mrs. Wattly sniffed. "Well, Betty weren't

goin' ta fight nobody over Mistress Stanford's jewels. That woman — begging yer pardon, miss — but that woman was a cruel one, mean ta my Betty she was."

She stared at me, her seamed face creased with pain. "My Betty was kilt 'cause o' somethin' she knew. I don't know what it was, but that's the truth o' it." Burying her face in her handkerchief she gave way to sobs.

We waited till she got control of herself again. "Sorry, miss," she said finally.

Behind me I could hear Archie shuffling his feet. I stood up. "We have to go now," I said, reaching down to pat her thin shoulder. "I have a few things that need mending. Arch— Lord Barrington will send a footman round with them."

Mrs. Wattly got to her feet, too.

"And here," Archie said, stepping around me. "You'll be needing a bit of money to buy thread and such." He glanced toward the hearth. "And coals for the fire."

Mrs. Wattly stared at the coins. "But, milord, 'tis too —"

"Nonsense," Archie said, cutting off her protest. "When the work is finished, you'll get the other half." And he pulled my arm through his and marched me out.

We lost no time getting into his carriage

and away from there. As soon as we were settled, I turned to smile at him. "You're a kind man, Archie."

He colored up and tried to look the other way. "Nonsense," he said. "I was just trying to impress you."

"You did that," I replied. "But I don't believe that was your reason for helping her."

He looked away for an instant. "I lost my older brother last year. I know what it's like to lose someone close."

I squeezed his arm. "I'm sorry."

He managed a small smile then looked anxious. "You do have something to send to her, don't you, Kate? That's why —"

"Don't worry, Archie. I'll find something." I grinned. "She'll have work even if I have to rip out some seams myself."

Archie grinned back at me. "You're a kind woman, Kate."

I shook my head. "Not really. It's just that I know what it's like to be cold and hungry."

For a minute Archie stared at me, almost like he thought I was joking, then he evidently realized I wasn't. Sobering, he patted my hand. "Never again," he said solemnly.

I felt a lump come up in my throat. "Don't be silly," I said, swallowing hard. "I told you Papa doesn't approve of keeping. He wants me to be a great tragic actress famous for my Lady Macbeth."

Archie tried really hard but he couldn't hold back his smile at the thought of me doing Lady Macbeth, and so the serious moment passed, as I meant it to, but of all the offers I've had, Archie's was by far the nicest.

CHAPTER THREE

That afternoon when I got back to the theater I went directly to my costumes. I didn't have a great many and Mama always saw they were kept in good condition, so there was very little to be fixed. That didn't bother me, though. A pile of clothes on my table, I set about opening seams and loosening hems — just little things, but plenty of them. I wanted enough work to justify the coins Archie had given Mrs. Wattly.

I was ripping the seam up the back of my red velvet breeches, very carefully of course since I needed them for the breeches parts I'd soon be doing, when Mama came in. If Papa had seen me busy doing such a thing, he would have yelled first and asked his questions later. But Mama just pushed some play books off the battered wooden chair and sat down. She watched me rip out a few more stitches, then said quietly, "All right, Kate, tell me what you're about."

I told her simply with none of the fancy embroidery I'd have put to a tale meant for Papa's ears. When I was done she nodded wisely. "That was well done of you, my dear. The poor woman can use your help." Then she frowned. "But this Lord Barrington, Kate, is he —" Her expression changed, almost embarrassed. She looked away, suddenly interested in the window across the room. "That is, do you —"

Usually Mama didn't beat about the bush, but she was always delicate about matters between men and women.

"Don't worry, Mama," I assured her with a little smile. "I've already turned Archie down. He's a good sort and he's helping Betty's mother. He's sending his footman to take these things to her and he's paying her to sew for me."

Mama got to her feet. "That's kind of him." She looked at me, her expression serious. "You're a grown woman, Kate. I won't say more. Just have a care."

I got up and gave Mama a good hug, following her to the door of the cramped little dressing room to watch her go down the dark narrow passageway. At the end she turned to wave at me and, smiling, I waved back.

Just as I was about to turn to search once

more through my things for anything else to send poor Mrs. Wattly, I heard the sound of voices from the room next door. Nell had a visitor. The voices grew louder, angrier. Plainly someone was put out with Nell, or she with him, I thought, since one of the voices sounded deep enough to be a man's.

When I heard the stamp of angry boots crossing the wooden floor, I drew back, not wanting her visitor to see me. Many actresses met admirers in the greenroom during and after performances, and some even invited them to their dressing rooms, but few encouraged daytime visitors. It was against Mr. Kemble's rules.

Of course, if the visitor were a peer, Mr. Kemble couldn't afford to antagonize him. Generally speaking, lords came and went as they pleased.

I drew back a little more, pulling my door almost closed, but curiosity kept me at the crack, watching. A tall man with black hair came out wearing the most elegant clothes and boots that shone even in the dim passageway. I caught a glimpse of his face as he went past. It was a hard face, cold as the marble sculpture outside the theater, a haughty face twisted into a fierce frown, but still very handsome and compelling in its arrogance.

I drew back even further, holding my breath. Now that was a real lord! A person could see that just by looking at him. What, I wondered, did such a gentleman want with a shrew like Nell?

Slowly I let out the breath I'd been holding. He walked with the confidence of the born aristocrat expecting the world to automatically move out of his way.

After he was out of sight, I turned again to my costumes. Nell wouldn't fancy me mooning over her admirer, but I couldn't help wondering who he was.

Perhaps Lavinia would know the man's name. She wasn't much of a gossip, but I'd soon discovered that if there was anything worth learning, Lavinia knew it.

Othello was playing that night and I'd rather hoped Mrs. Siddons might return to her role. Lavinia had said she did that sometimes, but it looked like the audience was doomed to hear Nell again.

Later, after Archie's footman had been dispatched to Fleet Street, his arms loaded with my manufactured mending, I went out to stand in the wings, watching Nell and Lavinia run through the scene where Othello is discovered by Emilia right after he's smothered Desdemona.

Mr. Kemble was busy about some other theater business and Peter was very poorly reading Othello's lines.

"Out and alas!" cried Lavinia, in what I thought were quite appropriate tones.

"No, no!" shrieked Nell, scrambling to her knees on the bed where she was supposed to lay dying. "Not like that! You must sound mournful."

"I do," Lavinia protested, obviously taken by surprise.

"You sound," Nell said scornfully, "like a sick cow — a sick cow *lowing*."

When I saw Lavinia swallow and bury her fists in her skirts, I knew she was fighting to control her temper. I wouldn't have taken Nell's tongue-lashing at all.

When Lavinia remained silent, Nell went on. "You must say it like this. O-o-o-u-t a-a-a-nd a-a-a-las."

And then Lavinia *couldn't* take any more. "It's my part!" she cried, putting her hands on her hips. "I've played it these many years without the slightest help from the likes of you!"

"Played it all wrong," Nell said caustically, scrambling out of her deathbed like some wrathful ghost. "Played it like the rawest provincial!"

"A fine one you are to be telling *me,*"

Lavinia cried, her voice rising almost to a shriek. "You play Desdemona like a — a — watering can, a *leaking* watering can!"

"I — don't — either!" Nell grabbed up a vase from the bedside table.

"Throw it!" Lavinia dared. "Go ahead, throw it why don't you!"

And Nell did. Lavinia ducked, of course, and it crashed against the flat that served as a back wall, shattering into pieces.

The next thing I knew Lavinia and Nell were at each other, tearing hair and costumes, finally falling to the floor in a tangle of arms and legs.

"Strumpet! Slut! Whore!" Nell shrieked, trying to scratch Lavinia's eyes out.

Lavinia was the heavier, though, and she rolled over, pinning Nell to the floor.

"I'll *kill* you!" Nell sobbed. "You mealy-mouthed, lumbering — cow!"

"Not if I get to you first!" Lavinia screamed. "You'll be the dead one then!"

"Stop! Stop this instant!" Mr. Kemble's deep bellow made them both freeze. "That is certainly enough!" He looked down at them severely. "Remember, you are professionals. Actresses, not fishwives!"

"Yes, sir," Lavinia said, climbing to her feet and smoothing down her costume. One sleeve hung loose and there was a big rip down the side of her skirt that she held together with one hand.

Nell leaped up and flounced out, her torn nightdress flapping. We all knew that though Mr. Kemble might reprimand her, he wouldn't dismiss her. He needed her to play Desdemona.

Still frowning, Lavinia came toward me. "You were fine," I whispered, reaching out to press her arm sympathetically. "I've never heard a better Emilia and I've heard a lot."

She smiled. "Thanks, Kate. I don't know what's wrong with Nell today. I shouldn't let her get to me, but she's even more tetchy than usual."

I nodded. "Maybe it's losing Betty like she did. Has she found a new dresser yet?"

"I saw several girls come through today. I think she took one of them on."

"Why doesn't she get someone older, someone more experienced?"

Lavinia laughed, her good nature restored. "Can you imagine an experienced dresser putting up with all that screaming? Nell had to get someone young, someone raw."

"Does she always throw things?" I asked, thinking of poor Betty again.

Lavinia nodded. "I'm afraid so." She patted my arm. "Listen, I'm going to go get a drink of water before *she* comes back."

I was just thinking of returning to my dressing room when Peter's hand came down on my shoulder. "That Nell," he said, "what an actress!"

I turned, easing out from under his hand. For a minute I wished that tall dark lord was there to put Peter in his place, to teach him with one cold look to keep his hands to himself.

"What do you mean?" I demanded, suddenly realizing that his tone had held admiration for Nell!

Peter smiled and any sensible woman would have backed away. "I mean Nell was right. Lavinia was doing a miserable job. Nell's a better actress than Mrs. Siddons."

I could hardly believe my ears. What had happened to Peter's judgment? Even the rankest amateur would know better than that. Unless . . . I looked carefully around. "Better not let Mr. Kemble hear you say that! You know how he feels about his sister's reputation as an actress."

Peter glanced around hastily, but seeing that Mr. Kemble was nowhere in sight, he stuck out his chest in that pompous way he had. "She's the best, Nell is," he said confidently. "We were talking about it just last night."

He emphasized last night, as though it

37

meant something significant.

Was I hearing this right? Peter and Nell? "You can't mean . . ."

He grinned. "Yes, I do. Nell and I —" He actually seemed to swell. "We have an agreement."

I still couldn't believe it. "Sure," I mocked. "And that lord that was in her dressing room this afternoon is her great-uncle! You and Nell — a likely story!"

Peter's face darkened. "You're wrong about the earl. Nell loves me. There's no one else."

Peter liked to jeer at others, but he didn't like being laughed at himself. I grinned.

Peter's florid face got redder and he stalked off. Lucky for me he hadn't asked what I thought of his reading of Othello. That would really have made him angry.

The days went by, busy days in which Archie became a comfortable part of my life. I could hardly remember what life in London had been like before I met him. Sometime he would have to return to his estate in the country but that seemed far in the future.

A week later I was in my dressing room as usual in time for the evening performance. Archie hadn't come backstage, but I knew he'd be in his box that evening and would come back to the greenroom to see me. He wasn't as grand as Nell's admirer, but he wasn't old or fat or ugly like a lot of the men who came backstage. And besides, he was fun.

That evening the play went on without a hitch. Though I had no part, I put on a new gown — one that Betty's mother had repaired — and went into the principal greenroom to mingle with the others. Nell came in to wait there between scenes and at the end of the play that admirer of hers strode in. I held my breath as he surveyed the room with those arrogant eyes, but his glance went right over me. To a man like that I was less than dirt — dirt might muck up his fine breeches — but I would never get that close.

Archie came in while I was standing there wishing like an idiot that I had sable hair and a big bosom like Nell's, and that that lord would . . . "Kate!" Archie cried in his cheerful voice, "my darling Kate." And he came toward me as though no one else was in the room. "Hello, love. Say, when are you going to act in something again? I miss seeing you."

I forgot my silly daydreams. "Soon. I'm in *The Constant Couple.*"

When he tucked my arm through his, I let it stay there. It was a harmless enough action and it pleased him.

"I'll be looking forward to it," he said, gazing down at me as though I were especially appetizing.

"Yes, Archie," I said, patting his arm. Sometimes his admiration was a little embarrassing, but having him beside me kept other admirers away. "But listen, do you know that man over there? The one talking to Nell?"

Archie turned to look, then swung back to me, making a disgusted face. "That's Lord Foxcroft," he said. "Best tell your friend Nell to be careful."

"Why?" I asked, my curiosity so getting the better of me that I didn't bother to tell him that Nell was not a friend.

Archie actually blushed, turning almost as red as the velvet breeches I'd sent to be mended. "He — the truth is the man has a reputation with women."

"Archie." I didn't mean to laugh at him but he really was funny. "Archie, didn't *you* offer to set me up?"

Archie looked startled. "Of course, you know I did, but that — that was different."

"How?" I asked in my most innocent tones.

"Well, because I really would take care of

you. And, and I wouldn't have you if I had a wife."

Archie certainly had a different code of honor than most men who, married or not, thought nothing of keeping a mistress.

"So the earl is married."

Archie nodded. "Yes, Kate. To a beautiful young woman." He glanced across the crowded room. "She's frail and blonde, much lovelier than Nell."

"And me," I muttered under my breath.

But Archie heard me. "No, Kate," he said with that engaging grin. "No one is lovelier than you."

I shook my head. "Be sensible, Archie. I'm not lovely. Not at all."

"You are to me."

He said it so simply, so honestly, that I didn't know how to reply without hurting his feelings, so instead I looked across the room to Nell and her aristocratic admirer. Nell's back was to me so I couldn't see her expression, but Lord Foxcroft was facing me. I've never seen a haughtier expression. Maybe he'd found out about Peter. If he wasn't careful, Peter was going to get himself into trouble. News travels fast in the theater, and his boasting to me about Nell might have been heard by someone else.

I just couldn't see Nell being interested in Peter. She must be using him for something. Was she in danger of losing Foxcroft to his lovely wife or some other woman? Maybe she hoped Peter would make the earl jealous, though that thought was ridiculous.

Just then Peter appeared in the doorway of the greenroom and struck a pose, but when he spotted Nell and Foxcroft together, his smile changed to a frown.

"Archie," I whispered, "look at that. Peter's going to make a fuss about Nell."

Archie frowned. "The fool, tangling with Foxcroft."

CHAPTER FOUR

Peter stood in the doorway for a few minutes, a frown on his face, then he pulled his shoulders back and started across the crowded room.

As always, each actor and actress had collected a little group of admirers and was basking in the attention, but Peter had no time for that. He didn't even nod as he made his way past people. He just kept heading straight for Nell.

Since her back was still to me, I couldn't see her face but Lord Foxcroft's dark features remained set in a haughty expression. Strange that such an expression could be attractive, yet it was.

Just before he reached Nell, Peter seemed to falter. For a minute, I thought he'd regained his senses and was going to turn away but he didn't.

It was a foolish thing for him to do. Poor

Peter must really be smitten by that shrew Nell.

"The idiot," Archie whispered. "Foxcroft will have his head."

"Shhh." I wanted to hear what Peter had to say, but there were so many people in the room, so much noise, that I could barely hear what Archie was saying to me, let alone make out the words of someone across the room.

"Kate," Archie began, "let me —"

"Hush! What are they saying?" I stared intently across the room, but I couldn't hear a word. I could see though, and what I saw didn't bode well for Peter. That foolish fellow marched right up and stuck his face close to Lord Foxcroft's.

I nudged Archie and drifted that way, trying to look nonchalant.

Archie must have guessed my intention. "Kate!" he protested, holding back as I tried to tug him past Lavinia and her newest admirer. "I really think —"

"Yes, Archie," I said cheerfully, maneuvering him still closer to where Nell stood with Foxcroft. "We're doing *The Constant Couple* — a great comedy."

Keeping my back to them, I came to a stop as close to Nell as I dared. That way I hoped they wouldn't know I was listening.

I rattled on, pretending to be talking to Archie, but actually listening as hard as I could to catch what was being said behind me.

"She can't go anywhere with you!" Peter protested, his voice hoarse with emotion. "We're in love, we're going to be married!"

I heard Nell's sharp intake of breath. "Nonsense, Peter!" she said shrilly. "I never said anything like that!"

Archie was plucking anxiously at my sleeve. I knew he wanted me to move away, but I ignored him and babbled on about the next role I was going to play.

Finally I paused for breath, and just in time, because a deep menacing voice from behind me said, "What I pay for belongs to me. Nell, I suggest you remember that."

Across from me, Archie's face paled, but I resisted the urge to turn and look at what he was seeing over my shoulder. And then I didn't have to. Lord Foxcroft crossed in front of me and headed toward the door, moving in his arrogant way, so that people automatically stepped out of his path. I let out the breath I hadn't known I was holding.

"Oh Nell," Peter was crying behind me, "how could you do this to me? You promised — You told me —"

"You're a fool, Peter Rutherford!" Her voice could have cut glass and I could only imagine the anger on her face.

"But I love you," Peter protested. "And you said you loved me!"

"Love!" Nell cried. "What earthly good is love? Get away from me, Peter. I don't want any more to do with you! Ever."

She made her exit, head high, expression disdainful. I got a glimpse of her face when she swept by us and I felt sorry for Peter.

Behind me Peter muttered a curse. "You'll be sorry for this, Nell. You'll be sorry."

I started to turn toward him, but Archie grabbed my arm and dragged me off.

"But Peter needs —" I began, setting my heels.

"No," Archie said firmly. "Trust me. A man doesn't appreciate compassion at a time like this. You'll only make him feel worse."

I didn't quite understand how that could be, but since Archie was a man and I wasn't, I let him have his way.

Archie and I stayed in the greenroom a while longer but I didn't go near Peter. Eventually he went out, threading his way through the little groups. A couple people

46

spoke to him, but he acted like he didn't hear them.

It was really terrible of Nell to treat Peter so shabbily. I certainly didn't like the forward way he had of putting his hands on me, but I liked Nell's behavior even less. It was an awful thing to trifle with someone's affections, to use a man, and then discard him.

Of course, men like Foxcroft used women all the time. They paid for what they got, though, and often there were no affections on either side. In that situation a wise woman would put something away for a rainy day.

But that kind of thing was for other women, not me. It was easy to defend the castle when no one like Foxcroft was attacking. Besides, I had better things to do with my life. I was my own person. I would never be the great tragic actress Papa wanted me to be. Even my love for him couldn't make me succeed at that. I belonged to the theater and in a breeches part I was among the best.

I had plans, goals. I meant to become as well known as the great Peg Woffington had been the century before. Some day young actresses would talk about me, would study how I played my parts, would hope to be as good as I was. At least, that was my dream.

"Kate," Archie said, pulling plaintively at my sleeve. "Come back to me."

"What? Oh, Archie, I'm sorry. What were you saying?"

"I was saying maybe we should go to your dressing room."

"Why?"

"Because it's late and you're tired."

There was something about the way he was looking at me, so tender like that it made me wonder what he was thinking.

"Very well," I said, "but Archie, you do understand — when I said no — I meant no, really no."

Archie smiled. "Kate, love, have no fear." He patted my arm, giving me another look that meant he was going to say something that would put a lump in my throat. "I respect your wishes. I'll always respect your wishes."

I swallowed the lump and took Archie's arm. "Then, let's go."

As we passed Nell's dressing room, I glanced that way. Was Lord Foxcroft in there with Nell? Or was Peter waiting for her, ready to promise her anything?

Archie reached around me to open my dressing room door. He was like that, always doing some nice little thing.

Crash! Bang!

Archie jerked back and looked at me. The noise had come from Nell's dressing room.

I shrugged. "Nell's throwing things again. She does it all the time. Yells, too. I pity that new dresser of hers."

Archie didn't smile. "A bad-tempered woman, that Nell."

"Yes, you know —"

Another bang came from Nell's dressing room and I made a face. We went into my room and I closed the door.

"Archie," I said, clearing off the chair for him, "Peter was really hurt by what Nell said . . ."

Archie sat down. "Yes," he said thoughtfully, "he was. But to tangle with Foxcroft. That was foolish."

"I suppose so." Foxcroft was arrogant but he had such presence I could understand why Nell or any woman would. . . .

"Aieeh!" The scream caught me just as I was settling onto my bench; it lifted Archie clean off the chair.

"Next door!" he cried, and he tore out, me right after him.

Just as we reached the hall, Nell's new dresser, Mary, came staggering out of her dressing room. Both hands to her mouth, she stared at us in wide-eyed horror.

49

"What is it?" Archie asked. "What's wrong?"

She shuddered, then pointed back at the room.

Archie looked at me then started past the cowering girl. He was halfway into Nell's dressing room when he called, "Kate, go back!"

Of course I didn't. I went in and there on the floor lay Nell, a scarf twisted tight around her neck. The moment I saw her I knew but I had to ask. "Is she —"

Archie knelt beside her. He nodded. "She's dead, Kate. Better send that girl for Kemble."

I started for the door but Mary had already gone. I could hear her calling down the hall. I leaned against the doorframe while waves of sickness washed over me. It was like a terrible nightmare, one that kept repeating itself. First Betty and now Nell, both of them strangled.

I tried not to look toward Nell. Her beautiful sable hair had come unpinned and straggled around her face, a face that was all purple and blotchy. If Peter saw her like that, he would never —

Peter! Peter had been so angry. Had he killed Nell, strangled her in rage over her betrayal?

I shivered, for a minute wishing I was back playing in the provinces. There the most worrisome thing we had to deal with was hecklers in the audience or perhaps not enough audience to guarantee our supper.

Archie got up and came to me. "Are you all right, Kate?"

Afraid to speak, I just nodded.

"Bit of bad luck, you seeing both of them like that."

He turned me around. "You go back in your dressing room, love, and wait there for me. Leave the door open." He looked around. "I'll find something to cover her. Shouldn't leave her like that."

If anyone else had sent me out I'd probably have argued, but I had no great liking for dead bodies, and besides, my knees were shaking.

So I went into my dressing room and sank down on my bench, my knees still weak and my hands still trembling. I left the door open and faced it. No one was going to sneak up behind me.

It wasn't long before the corridor began to fill with people. Mr. Kemble came and hurried into Nell's room. Papa was right behind him, but he came into my room instead, stopping just inside the door.

"Now, Kate," he said, trying to gentle his

51

usual boisterous voice. "What's this about another body?"

"It's true, Papa. Archie and I found her. That is, we went in after we heard her new dresser scream."

Papa frowned, shaking his leonine head. "A terrible thing. It'll give the theater a bad name. You mark my word, my girl, it'll be all over London. Thank God the great Siddons wasn't here tonight."

I stared at him. What did Mrs. Siddons have to do with this? "Why, Papa?"

He gave me a disbelieving look. "Kate, Kate. Two dead women. Two! Mrs. Siddons can't be put in such danger."

Danger? "But Papa, what makes you think there's any connection to her?"

Papa thrust out his chest and put on what he called his tragic muse. "Death!" he cried dramatically. "Death comes for Desdemona."

I thought death had come for quite a lot of other people, too, but I didn't say so. I never contradicted Papa.

Papa came closer. "You must be careful, Kate." He frowned. "I don't like you being here, so close, and two dead women found right next door."

I was liking it less and less myself, but I couldn't do anything about it. The Bow

Street Runners would be coming to investigate. And no doubt that Constable Kennedy would have some notion to put forward. Surely he wouldn't suspect a robber this time. My mind raced. Two murders — both women strangled. Could this murder have anything to do with Betty's? What? I remembered Betty's mother, her face twisted with grief, telling me that Betty had been afraid. And this afternoon, Nell had been so touchy, even worse than usual. Could there be some connection?

Papa reached into his pocket. "Your mother sent you this." He held out Mama's favorite ornament, a pewter Celtic brooch, a circle about an inch in diameter, from which suspended a pin some two inches long. "Your mother says to wear this on your bodice, keep it with you at all times. If you're in any trouble, any trouble whatsoever, you stab whatever you can rcach."

I almost laughed at Papa, delivering himself of such a message in such overly tragic tones. But I had no desire to be lying dead on the floor with a scarf around my neck. So I took the brooch and slipped it into the bosom of my gown where it would be easy to reach. It did make me feel a little safer knowing it was there.

Papa gave me a majestic nod and went

out to see what Mr. Kemble was doing, no doubt. Soon Archie came, leaning in the doorway. "You look better," he said. "A little more color to your cheeks. But I'm afraid we aren't done with this yet."

"I know. The Bow Street Runners are coming."

Archie smiled and offered me his arm. I took it gratefully, relieved he was there, but of course I didn't tell him so.

CHAPTER FIVE

The same Constable Kennedy and his subordinates assembled the company in the greenroom again. We pushed the red velvet chairs in a semicircle with the constable in the middle and a man posted at the door. Archie took the chair beside me and leaned close, holding my hand in his. I didn't really need comforting, but it was still good to have him there. Across the room, Mama and Papa sat together — Papa frowning fiercely and Mama looking her usual serene self.

"Now," Constable Kennedy said, puffing out his chest — the more I saw of him the more he reminded me of a little bantam rooster strutting up and down before us. "This 'ere puts a whole new face on the situation. Someone's done this 'un in, too. The question is why — why'd they do it?"

He looked around the circle as though he expected us to give him the answer, but everyone just stared back at him blankly.

Constable Kennedy questioned each of us in turn. And all the time he was talking I was wondering if it could have been Peter who strangled Nell. It hardly seemed possible, but he had been very upset with her and Foxcroft. And he was young and strong.

"Now," Constable Kennedy said, fixing his bulging eyes on Peter. "When'd ye last see the dead woman?"

Peter's face was ashen. "I —" He moistened his lips and looked at me and then at Archie. "In the greenroom. After the play." He gulped and struggled on. "You see, we — we were — going to get married."

The constable nodded, trying to arrange his ruddy features into an expression of sympathy. "Married, is it? Go on."

Peter wiped awkwardly at his eyes with the back of his hand. "We — we had an argument."

"Oh?" The constable's look said volumes. " 'Bout what?"

"She — I —" Peter searched for words. "She was with someone else," he stumbled on. "And — and she said she didn't mean to marry me." I never saw a more piteous face on a man than Peter's at that moment. "We quarreled."

"Did anyone else see this quarrel?" the constable asked.

Archie nodded. "I did," he said.

The constable turned. "And ye are?"

Archie straightened, suddenly looking the lord he was. "Archibald Islington, Viscount Barrington. Miss Ketterling's friend."

The constable bobbed his head respectfully. "I've seen ye 'ere afore, milord — when t'other was murdered."

Archie frowned. "Yes, I was here. As I said, I am Miss Ketterling's friend." He glanced toward Peter. "It happened just as Mr. Rutherford told you. We heard part of the argument, saw most of it."

I nodded. "That's right, constable. After that we stayed in the greenroom for a while and then we went to my dressing room."

Constable Kennedy frowned. "Ye and 'is lordship here?"

I knew what he was thinking — that Archie was my particular friend, the man who *kept* me. "Yes," I said, avoiding Papa's glower. Evidently that's what he was thinking, too. "Because of the murder of poor Betty, you see, his lordship didn't want me to be alone there this evening."

For the moment the constable looked almost fatherly. "So, miss, do ye know anymore 'bout this nasty business?"

I shook my head. "No, constable, I don't."

The constable whirled on Peter. "So ye

had a quarrel?"

"Y-yes," Peter stammered. He looked truly miserable. "But Nell didn't mean it. I know she didn't. I knew she'd be sorry."

I stiffened. The very words I'd heard Peter mutter after the argument!

"Well," Constable Kennedy frowned portentously, "looks bad for ye, Mr. Rutherford — the two of ye havin' that fight."

Peter jumped to his feet, his face going white. "But I didn't do it!" He looked around. "There's someone else with a reason to kill Nell."

Beside me I heard Archie's sharp intake of breath. Surely Peter wouldn't try to put the blame on Lord Foxcroft. So what if Nell and her protector had had words. Nell had words with everyone.

"Her!" Peter said, pointing an accusing finger, and startling us all. "Lavinia Patrick wanted Nell dead. Why, just this afternoon they had a terrible fight! Everyone saw it. And Lavinia threatened to kill Nell!"

Constable Kennedy turned to Lavinia. "That true?" he asked.

Lavinia looked surprised, but not fearful. "Yes, constable," she admitted, giving him back look for look. "Nell insulted me during rehearsal in front of everyone. She — well, we fought. And she threatened me. But

58

I didn't kill her. I didn't kill anyone."

Lavinia's dark features made her look fierce, dangerous even, but I knew she was a kind person, a good person. "Constable," I said, "just a minute. Don't you think that maybe there's a connection to Betty's murder?"

"Betty?" He looked like he'd never heard the name before.

"The maid who was murdered in this same room. Last week."

The constable scowled. "That were pure robbery. Don't worry yerself 'bout it, miss. If there's a connection, we'll find it."

"But," I insisted, "it seems to me that —"

He gave me a hard look. "Now miss, ye're a pretty enough little thin' and a fair actress, too. I've seen ye." He smiled so briefly I almost missed it. "But you don't know nothin' 'bout solving crimes. So kindly leave that to them as does."

I opened my mouth to protest that *them as does* weren't doing any solving, at least of Betty's case, but the pressure of Archie's fingers on mine stopped me from speaking. I knew what he meant to tell me. It was useless to argue.

The constable looked around the circle. "Don't any of ye be leavin' London, now."

Mr. Kemble cleared his throat. "I assure

you, constable, my people will be here. The play must go on, you know. Mistress Patrick will be needed to take Mistress Stanford's parts."

The constable frowned. "Is that so now?" He eyed Lavinia. "Leading parts, too, no doubt."

Lavinia looked more shocked than she had when the constable questioned her about the murder. Her eyes wide, she faced Mr. Kemble. "Me? Play Desdemona?"

Mr. Kemble nodded. "Yes, we can't cancel any performances —"

"But Mr. Kemble, how can I? I've never played Desdemona . . ."

Mr. Kemble drew himself up to his full height, and an imposing picture he made, with his noble face so serious and somber. "You will play the part."

Poor Lavinia. She couldn't say no to Mr. Kemble, but it was obvious she didn't want the part, obvious to everyone but the constable. He went on looking thoughtful, which in his case meant scowling and thrusting out his lower lip. Then he said, "Well, it 'pears I'll 'ave to take ye both afore the magistrate."

Peter turned red. "Arrested? But —"

"I ain't sayin' arrested — yet." Constable Kennedy looked officially inscrutable.

60

"That's up to the magistrate, not me. Now ye just come along."

Peter drew back, his eyes frantic. "This — this is impossible! I didn't kill Nell! I loved her."

Constable Kennedy wasn't impressed. " 'Fraid that don't signify. Love makes a man behave peculiar."

The Runners moved over to stand beside Peter. He looked like he wanted to bolt but there was no chance. Two men were beside him and another stood by the door.

Lavinia sighed, got wearily to her feet, and let the men lead her out.

"Poor Lavinia!" I grabbed Archie's arm. "We can't let them —"

He patted my hand. "Don't worry, love. You go home. I'll find out what the magistrate has to say."

"Archie, can you —"

"Shhh," he said, giving me a hard look that told me plainly not to say any more. "Just let me handle this. You run along home."

I didn't want to run along anywhere. And I certainly didn't like Archie treating me like a foolish girl. But I had to face facts. The magistrate would listen to Archie, but wasn't likely to listen to an actress, and one not even famous at that. I swallowed my frustration and did the sensible thing. "Thank you, Archie."

The next morning when Archie came round to our rooms, I hurried into my bonnet and cloak before Papa could object. "The magistrate let them both go," Archie told me as we strolled down the crowded street toward Covent Garden Market, "but they haven't really given up. I think Kennedy still believes Lavinia might have done it."

I almost snorted. "Oh Archie, Lavinia couldn't kill anyone. That Kennedy couldn't find his own head! How did he get to be —"

Archie laughed. "I guess being a Bow Street Runner isn't the world's easiest job. Probably doesn't attract the smartest people either. I spoke to the magistrate. Kennedy hasn't convinced him of Lavinia's guilt, so the magistrate hasn't committed her for trial."

"MURDER MOST 'ORRIBLE," a street crier yelled, almost in my ear. "Actress kilt, strangled dead. Only 'alf a penny. Read all about it."

"No," Archie said. And when the street crier waved his papers under my nose, Archie snapped. "Enough! Go sell to someone else!"

Archie looked almost fierce and the poor man hurried off, shouting "Murder Most 'Orrible."

Archie's frown became a scowl. "All London's talking about these murders, you know."

I nodded. "There's got to be some connection between them. I know it. Betty and her fellow, Wild Man Willie, are involved somehow. But Constable Kennedy won't listen to me."

Archie pressed my arm sympathetically. "It's too bad there's no one to search out the real killers. Someone with some sense, someone who'll look at all the facts."

I stopped so suddenly that several people narrowly avoided crashing into us from behind. I almost got shoved into the kennel which, since it was full of foul-smelling water, would not have been pleasant. I grabbed Archie's arm. "Archie, you marvelous man, that's it!"

Archie stared at me, his fair face reddening in confusion, his moustache twitching. "Kate, whatever are you talking about?"

"*We'll* do it. We'll find the killer!"

Archie's jaw dropped almost to his waistcoat. "Kate! You can't be serious! We don't know anything about finding murderers."

He was right, of course, but I didn't

intend to admit it. "Perhaps not," I said, strolling on. "But we know more than that Constable Kennedy does. We know Lavinia isn't guilty. And we know there must be some connection between the two murders. We just have to find it."

Archie pulled anxiously at his cuff. "We *think* there's a connection, Kate, we don't know it. Really, this kind of thing won't wash. And it might be dangerous."

"Posh!" I said. "How can it be dangerous? No one will know we're even looking." I leaned my bosom against his arm, just a little, and smiled up into his face. "It'll be an adventure. And we can do it together."

"Kate, really, I don't think — Together, you say?"

I could almost see Archie's mind working. But was it my fault if he thought he could change my mind about that "pretty little establishment" he'd offered? I wasn't making any promises. I just wanted his help; I wanted him to continue being my friend. With Archie at my side, I could go anywhere in London. Alone it would be much more difficult.

I didn't wait for him to have second thoughts. "We'll go talk to Mrs. Wattly again this afternoon. Maybe she can tell us something." I squeezed his arm. "Oh Archie, you're such a dear."

We took Archie's closed carriage to the alley off Fleet Street where Mrs. Wattly lived. The fog was coming in, blanketing the city in yellow-gray cotton wool, and the stairs seemed even darker and drearier than before. The whole place had a terrible odor of dampness and decay about it, and something more I didn't want to think about, or put a name to.

"Miserable place to live," Archie muttered glumly, echoing my thought exactly. "Can't see how they can stand it. Ought to be torn down."

"Shhh, Archie. These buildings can't be torn down. Where would these people go?"

Mrs. Wattly opened the door before he could answer. "Miss Kate!" she cried. " 'Tis so good ta see you again." She motioned to us. "Do come in."

She glanced anxiously at my empty arms. " 'Ave you no mendin' fer me then? I was 'oping you'd be bringin' me more. I finished the last lot this mornin'." She motioned me to the only chair.

In all the confusion, I hadn't thought about bringing her anything more to do. "No, Mrs. Wattly, I —"

Archie didn't wait for me to dredge up

lame excuses. "Kate and I have talked about this," he said, "and this is what we decided. We'd like you to sew just for Miss Kate."

Mrs. Wattly sank wearily onto the cot. "But milord, I don't know. Much as I'd like ta, I got ta make a livin'."

Archie put on his lordly look. "I know that. Of course it means you'll have to be ready at any time. So I intend to pay for all your time."

Mrs. Wattly looked startled. "But milord, if you pay and there's no work —"

Archie looked even more lordly. "If there's no work, you wait." Poor Mrs. Wattly — she was no match for Archie. "You hold yourself in readiness." He looked around the sparse little room, glancing at the hearth, still cold. "You see, Miss Kate might need something done at a moment's notice. So I want you to keep a fire on the hearth. Keep your fingers nimble."

Mrs. Wattly sighed. "There's nothin' I'd like better, milord, but the price o' coals —"

Archie looked aggrieved. "You'll be getting coals delivered."

"D— delivered?" Mrs. Wattly stammered, putting a hand to her heart in surprise.

Archie nodded. "The footman who brought the costumes will bring you coals.

Every day." Archie looked stern, a difficult task for him. "And you must use them. Keep this place warm."

"Yes, milord." Mrs. Wattly, finally perceiving what he was about, gazed up at him with something close to adoration. "You're a fine man, milord, a fine —"

"Nonsense," Archie said briskly, his fair cheeks slowly turning red. "This is a business arrangement."

Mrs. Wattly knew better. So did I. But since Archie obviously wanted nothing more said about it, we didn't pursue the matter. I leaned forward. "Mrs. Wattly, I wonder, would you mind telling us some more about Wild Man Willie?" I took a deep breath. "You see we're sure"— Archie frowned, not looking at all sure —"that is, we suspect that there's a connection between Betty's death and Nell Stanford's."

Mrs. Wattly frowned. "I 'eard that Mistress Stanford was kilt last eve, but I didn't think —" Her eyes widened. "You think the same person —"

"I think it's likely," I said. "But the Runners don't."

Mrs. Wattly frowned. She pulled the tattered shawl closer around her and shook her head.

"You mentioned Betty's fellow before —

Wild Man Willie his name is?"

"Aye. Poor Willie." Mrs. Wattly sniffed. " 'E's beside 'isself with grief. Can't 'ardly fight, 'e says."

"Do you know where we can find him?"

Archie made a protesting noise in his throat. Clearly he didn't like the idea of us looking for Willie. But Mrs. Wattly had said they'd argued. I wanted to know what they had argued about.

"When 'e's not trainin'," Mrs. Wattly said, " 'e goes round ta a tavern, the Cock and Bull."

"I know the place," Archie said, and his tone wasn't encouraging. "Filthy and — that is, it's not a fit place for a woman."

" 'Deed not," Mrs. Wattly agreed. "My Betty wouldn't go there."

Perhaps not but I intended to. I got to my feet. "Thank you, Mrs. Wattly."

She rose from the cot and came to press my hand. "You find 'em, Miss Kate. You find those villains what kilt my Betty. And you make 'em pay fer it!"

"I'll do my best, Mrs. Wattly," I said, pressing her frail hand in return. "I'll do my very best."

CHAPTER SIX

"No," Archie said as the carriage set off toward Covent Garden, "absolutely not! I won't take you to the Cock and Bull. How can you ask it? Why, that place is the worse kind of gin mill. It's out of the question."

"But Archie, dear Archie, don't you see? It'll be so easy."

"Easy?" Poor Archie looked about to explode. "I can't take a woman —"

"You won't have to."

Archie looked confused. "But you said —"

"I won't *be* a woman."

Archie stared at me, his face flushed and his usually warm eyes bewildered. "Kate, please, I don't understand this. Explain it to me."

I grabbed his arm. I'd already noticed that Archie responded to me best when I was touching him. "I'll just wear a pair of my breeches like I wear to act in. You can say I'm your cousin, fresh in from the country."

Archie looked down at my bosom, which at the moment was pressing against his arm, and his moustache twitched. "Kate, love, be reasonable. How can you hide that?"

Archie looked embarrassed just mentioning that part of my anatomy. "I'll just wear a big shirt and a waistcoat and coat," I said. "You'll see. I can look like a boy, a young man."

Archie didn't look convinced. I leaned a little closer. "Archie, please, just give me a chance to show you."

With me looking at him like that, there was no way he could resist. "Well, I —"

By that time we'd stopped outside the theater. "Come into my dressing room," I said, "and we'll talk about it."

I talked Archie into it, finally, by going behind the changing screen and emerging as a young man, complete with coat and cap. London's back streets are full of boys. No one paid them much mind.

I turned in a small circle so he could see me from every angle. "So, Archie, will I do?"

He looked like he'd eaten too many green apples, but all he said was, "I like you better in a gown."

"But I'll pass as a boy," I persisted. "You can't argue with that."

And Archie didn't argue. I put on a dark

hooded cloak to hide my clothes till we got to the carriage, and out we went.

The Cock and Bull was worse than filthy. The rough planking floor was littered with bits of food and gnawed bones. Acrid smoke hung in clouds in the air. How could Archie worry about anyone recognizing me in this haze? No one could even see me.

The noise beat against me like a living thing, worse than the racket the bullies in the pit make, worse than anything I'd ever heard.

Since I was wearing male clothes, I couldn't very well hang on Archie's arm, but I kept as close to him as I could get. In spite of my brave words, the place was doing awful things to my stomach.

All around us unwashed brutes swilled gin and bellowed at each other, every other word an obscenity. I had never seen so many disgusting people in one place. I strode along at Archie's side doing my best to swagger as a young boy might.

"Do you see him?" I asked, in what passed for a whisper in that incredible din.

"Maybe." Archie was obviously not happy and he wanted me to know it. "Just hold on."

While Archie strained his eyes to spot Wild

Man Willie in the murk that surrounded us, I concentrated on playing my role. I was a young lad out for an adventuresome evening. The smell of stale gin and countless unwashed bodies wasn't going to unsettle my stomach. If it did, I certainly wasn't going to let it show on my face.

I occupied my mind and tried to distract my stomach by looking around. My gaze met that of a man across the room — the dark lord who'd been Nell Stanford's last protector. For a long moment I felt mesmerized, but his gaze passed over me. I was nothing to him, just another low class ruffian. He turned to the man next to him, a fighter from the size of him, and I looked away.

Foxcroft looked out of place in that gin cellar. What was he doing here?

Slowly I let my gaze go back to his table. He sat with several men, grimy specimens, and another whose back was to me. Something familiar about that back made me pause, something . . . The man turned and I gasped. Peter! Peter Rutherford sitting there, drinking with a man he hated, a man who'd been his rival for Nell.

I drew back, trying to watch without them seeing me. If he felt me looking at him, Peter might recognize me even in this murk.

That would convince poor Archie that he'd been right about the danger all along, and effectively ruin our mission for the evening.

I inched around, putting Archie's body between me and the table where Lord Foxcroft and Peter sat, still managing to watch them. Shaking his head vehemently, Peter handed some money across the table to one of the fighters, an ugly fellow with a dirty red kerchief knotted at his throat. The man said something and Peter banged his tankard on the table, splattering gin. Lord Foxcroft simply raised a dark eyebrow and went on talking to the brute nearest him.

Peter stood up so violently that the bench behind him crashed to the floor, but the noise in the room was such that no one noticed. Peter raised a fist and shook it. Lord Foxcroft never moved. I wished I could hear what Peter was saying, but I doubted even the people at the next table could understand it. This time I knew better than try to get closer.

Peter shook his fist once more, then turned, and stumbled toward the door. From the way he lurched I could tell he was very drunk. I kept back, using Archie as a shield. Archie, still looking for Wild Man Willie, never noticed.

Peter was already out the door when Archie pulled at my sleeve. "C'mon. I see him."

As I followed Archie between the crowded tables, a barmaid came toward us, a blowsy creature with a grimy neck and a bosom that her stained blouse barely covered. She brushed against Archie when she went by him. His lip quivered with distaste but he pressed on.

The table we approached, of heavy battered oak, held the tankards of two men, both of them great hulking brutes.

"Evening, Willie," Archie said, in that hearty tone sporting men use with each other. He extended a hand to shake the man's huge paw.

"Evenin', milord." Willie peered through the haze. "Don't know this lad, do I?"

"This?" Archie's voice held a faint note of panic. When I kicked unobtrusively at his ankle, he gave me a look of reproach, then said, "This is my cousin, ah, Nick. New in from the country. Wants to see the sights of London."

I nodded emphatically and gazed around. I'd often wished to know the kind of place that Papa frequented when he went out with his drinking companions. Now I knew and wished I didn't.

"This 'ere's Bob. Bruising Bob 'e's called."

"Bob." Archie nodded. "Mind if we sit?" he asked, indicating the empty bench on our side of the table.

"Don't mind," said Bruising Bob, shrugging his huge shoulders.

We sat, Archie with a sigh of relief and me grateful to turn my back on the room.

While Archie engaged in small talk which I hoped would eventually lead to the subject I had in mind, I surveyed the two across from me. They were big men, their worn shirts strained over heavy shoulders and their faces showing the effects of much battering. One sported a misshapen ear and the other a nose that tended to lean off center. Obviously they were veterans of many fights, violent men whose huge fists had many times pounded other men.

And yet that day their faces were gentle. Willie heaved a sigh. "I ain't 'ad no mind ta fight," he was saying. "Ask Bob 'ere. I ain't got no spirit fer it."

" 'E's right there," Bob said, nodding his shaggy head in agreement.

Archie nodded in sympathy. "That was a terrible thing," he said. "Betty being — left like that. Too bad the Runners couldn't catch the cracksman that did it."

"Weren't no —" I had the distinct impression that Bob had pinched his companion under the table. At any rate, Willie stopped in mid-sentence and didn't go on.

After a few seconds, Archie said, "We — I —" He didn't look at me, but I knew he regretted that "we." "I was there that night," he went on, leaning so far across the table I could barely hear his words. "I don't believe it was robbery at all." He stared straight at Willie. "I think someone murdered poor Betty. And not by accident."

Wild Willie gave a wretched sob and rubbed at his eyes. It occurred to me that they were red from weeping, not from the stinging smoke that infested the place.

"I've been to see Betty's mother," Archie went on.

Willie swallowed. "She told me as 'ow you and the little actress done fer her. That was real kind."

"She told *me,*" Archie said, "that Betty was afraid of something. Or someone. Do you know what? Or who?"

Willie's face, until that moment full of open grief, suddenly became closed and furtive. His gaze darted anxiously about the room. "Afeard? She ain't had no cause ta be afeard o' nothin'."

He was lying. I was good at spotting such things and I knew it. Willie was scared and he was lying.

"Of course not," Archie said. "I just thought it was a possibility." He laid a coin on the table. "Let me pay for this round. I'd like to stay and have a drink with you. I hear Robson's going to meet Thicket again soon. But I've got to get this scamp home before daylight."

I followed Archie back across the room. Sneaking a look, I saw that the table where Foxcroft had sat now held different men. He was gone. But my mind was on other things. Why hadn't Archie pressed Willie for an answer? It was so plain Willie was lying. Betty had been afraid then. Willie was afraid now.

And there was something else. When Archie spoke of the coming match between Robson and Thicket, Willie and Bob had exchanged quick fearful glances. One or the other of those pugilists gave them cause for alarm.

I wanted to ask Archie if he'd heard the fear in Willie's voice, but I knew I'd better not talk where we might be overheard. Archie didn't look at all happy. His face had turned gray and he was plainly put out with me. I couldn't really blame him. I shouldn't have badgered him into taking me there. If I'd really known what it was like, I probably wouldn't have asked him at all.

So I just followed quietly along until we reached his carriage. Besides, I was busy breathing in incredibly fresh air after the fetidness of the Cock and Bull. In fact, I waited till the carriage was well away from the tavern before I opened my mouth. Then I took care to make my tone sweet.

"Thank you, Archie." I put a hand on his sleeve. "You were right," I said, leaning toward him just a little. "I've never seen such a dreadful place in my whole life. The noise! And the awful smell!"

Papa taught me to look for motive. Mama taught me to give thanks when it was due. Both lessons have stood me in good stead.

Archie's stony look gradually softened. "Knew it wasn't any place for a lady. Told you so."

I wasn't a lady but I appreciated the compliment. I gave him my best smile. "And you were right," I repeated. "But Archie, I'm curious, why didn't you make Willie tell you what he knew?"

Archie stared at me in surprise. "Make him! Me? Come, come, Kate. You saw the man. I couldn't make him do anything."

"Perhaps not," I conceded, leaning back against the squabs. "But he might have confided in you if you'd been more — more lordly."

"So that's it!" Archie eyed me in disgust. "You want me to act aristocratic and arrogant, like, like Foxcroft!"

I hadn't thought of it quite like that, but . . . "Well, yes, sort of."

Archie frowned. "It's true that most common men treat titles with deference. But Kate, love, some men, men like Wild Man Willie and Bruising Bob, they're rather used to dealing with aristocrats because of their interest in the Fancy, you see. And short of my employing someone to do them violence —"

A giggle escaped me and I covered my mouth with my hand. I couldn't imagine Archie hurting anyone — it was just too ridiculous.

Archie gave me a wounded look and I hastened to apologize. "I'm sorry, Archie, honest I am. I guess I'm still a little strung up. But I just can't imagine you hurting anyone."

"A person doesn't need to do it himself," Archie said grimly. "Anyone with enough blunt can find ready hands to hire."

I shivered a little. "That's dreadful, Archie. But we're getting off the subject. You do think Willie was frightened of something, don't you?"

"Of course. But the way to find out what is not by threats but by friendship."

"Then . . . Betty's mother!" I cried, light finally dawning.

"Betty's mother," Archie repeated approvingly. "She wants to see her daughter's killer brought to justice."

"Oh yes! Now I see! She'll prevail on Willie to tell us what he knows!"

"That's my hope," Archie said. He eyed me sternly. "But whether he does or not, I tell you right now, Kate Ketterling, I do not intend to take you to the Cock and Bull again!" He looked as though he expected me to protest such an ultimatum, but truthfully I had no desire to repeat that evening's visit.

Still, I couldn't resist teasing him just a little. "Really, Archie, it was not so bad. And no one even suspected me."

When Archie's expression started to turn thunderous, I feared I'd gone too far, so I added quickly, "Still, you're right. You know more about such things than I do."

Placated, Archie smiled at me. But he still hadn't mentioned that peculiar look I'd seen on Willie's face. "Archie, what do you know about those fighters — Robson and Thicket?"

Archie shrugged. "Not a lot. Both are good fighters." He frowned thoughtfully. "Wait. Now that I think of it, seems there was some kind of talk after their last fight."

I perked up. "Talk? What kind of talk?"

"Something about . . ." He looked thoughtful. "I remember now. There was a rumor that perhaps Robson's last fight had been fixed, a cross they call it. Probably nothing to it, though. Rumors like that are always going round. You can't pay much mind to them."

"Oh." No wonder Willie had looked upset. A pugilist who took a cross would make them all look bad. But that had nothing to do with Betty.

Archie looked at his pocket watch and sighed. "I suppose I have to take you home now."

"Yes," I said. "We should get there before Mama and Papa return from the theater. I don't want Papa to know where I've been."

Archie chuckled. "No, I should suppose not." He heaved a gigantic sigh. "You know, Kate, you are the unkindest creature."

I thought I knew what he was about but I pretended ignorance. "I? Unkind?"

"Yes, you!" Archie declared. "Here I am, absolutely mad about you, willing to offer you a pretty establishment of your own, and

81

more, anything your little heart desires." He shook his head ruefully. "And you refuse me to chase after murderers."

"I'm tired," I said plaintively. "I want to go home."

CHAPTER SEVEN

The next day, true to his word, Archie went off to see Mrs. Wattly again to ask her help in persuading Willie to tell us what he knew about his argument with Betty. Unfortunately, I couldn't go with him. We were getting ready to do Farquhar's *Constant Couple* in which I was playing Sir Harry Wildair. I already knew my part, of course. It was one of my best breeches parts and I was quite accomplished at it.

But no matter how good I was, I knew I couldn't miss rehearsals. The theater was more than just work to Mr. Kemble. It was his passion, his mistress so-to-speak, since he was too straitlaced to have a flesh and blood mistress. At any rate, I knew he'd be upset if I wasn't there for rehearsal.

I didn't want to disappoint Mr. Kemble but that wasn't all of it. Even more I didn't want to disappoint Papa. Actually, Papa had said very little about my gadding around town with Archie. It was true I was old enough to conduct my own life, but Papa was old-fashioned about certain things. Normally he would have made a big fuss about such behavior whether I was with a lord or not. Since Papa hadn't made a fuss, I suspected that Mama had had a good talk with him.

So there I was, swaggering around the stage in my breeches, pretending to be a man. The rakish Sir Harry Wildair said, "My Love is neither romantically honourable, nor meanly mercenary, 'tis only a pitch of Gratitude; while she loves me, I love her; when she desists, the Obligation's void." I almost frowned as I said the words. A rather poor sort of love, I thought, more like the business arrangement Nell had had with Foxcroft. I couldn't imagine feeling so coldly about Archie, even if he wasn't my protector.

Peter, playing the earnest upright soldier Standard, was throwing his lines out like the remains of yesterday's cold dinner. Twice I saw Mr. Kemble wince and shake his head at Peter's poor delivery.

But my mind wasn't entirely on my lines either. I kept seeing Peter as he'd been the night before, shaking his fist at Lord Foxcroft, and stumbling drunkenly out of the tavern. What had Peter said to Foxcroft? Could Peter still be claiming Nell had loved him?

Then I came to where Sir Harry said, "An honourable Lover is the greatest Slave in Nature; some will say the greatest Fool." Peter stared at me, his face turning bright red. He stood there, silent, while everyone waited, and for a long long moment, I thought he'd entirely forgotten his lines. Finally, though, he rallied and went on, more poorly than before. I wondered that Mr. Kemble didn't say something, but I guess he felt sorry for Peter.

When we reached the scene where Standard exclaims, "What is the Bane of Man, and Scourge of Life, but Woman?" Peter paused and swallowed hard. Again he stood silent for far too long. Finally he took a deep breath and forced the words out. "False deluding Woman . . . their Body's Heavenly, but their Souls . . . are . . . Clay." On the last word, he threw me an angry look and stumbled from the stage.

"That'll be all now," Mr. Kemble said in his deep voice. "Study your lines privately."

Minutes later I hurried along the dim narrow hall, a shiver slithering down my spine as I neared the door to Nell's dressing room, a door tightly closed. No one was using that room now and probably no one would for a long time. Theater folk are a superstitious lot. One murder is enough to put us off but two . . .

Thinking about those murders made me so nervous I couldn't make up my mind whether to close my dressing room door or leave it open. Finally I decided to leave it ajar just a little. I didn't like being in there alone.

Once, when the floor outside my door creaked, I pulled Mama's Celtic pin clear out of my bodice before I realized what I was doing. Since it was basically just a long, straight pin with no fastener on it, it slid out easily. Then I realized why she wanted me to wear it. Grasping the round head made the two inches of pin almost like a dagger. I sat there staring down at it in surprise.

Another creak in the hall brought my head erect. Still clutching the pin, I got slowly to my feet and edged toward the door. Someone was coming quietly down the hall. I'd heard no footsteps, only the creak. I reached the door and put my eye to the crack. Peter! He cast a quick look behind him and then slipped into Nell's dressing room. Why was he sneaking? What was he looking for in there?

Should I go knock on the door? Or perhaps tiptoe over and crack it open so I could see what he was doing? Peter was obnoxious sometimes, but would he really kill someone? Still I hesitated. Peter was a big man, strong, and I could be wrong about him. After all, there wasn't much point in discovering the murderer's identity just to become his next victim.

But I was strong, too, with a good pair of lungs and too much curiosity to stay safely in my dressing room. Clutching my pin, I eased out and along the dim hall. Peter hadn't quite closed Nell's door. I put my eye to the crack, but I couldn't see anything.

I leaned forward a little further. Still nothing. I could hear strange sounds, though. I had to see what he was doing. Slowly I extended a hand and gave the door the slightest push. It swung open a little. I gave it another push.

Then I could see Peter. His back was to me and he was rummaging through a pile of Nell's play books. I eased a step closer. If he found something in there, I wanted to see what it was.

Impelled by my curiosity, I took still another step, almost into the room. And the floorboard creaked under my foot. Peter whirled, his face gone white. "Kate! What are you doing here?"

"I — I heard a noise and I wondered who was in here." I decided boldness was my best attitude, and hiding the hand holding the pin in the folds of my skirt, I moved closer. "Are you looking for something? Maybe I can help."

Peter's eyes widened. "Looking for — Ah, it's just that Nell had something of mine." He looked around the room, avoiding my eyes. "Something I'd given her. And I want it back. A — a keepsake."

I moved toward her dressing table, examining the array of bottles and jars jumbled there. "Can't be perfume," I said, giving him my best innocent look. "Or clothes. Oh, I bet I know — it's a love letter."

His face paled even more, but he tried to put a good show on it, blustering. "Don't be silly, Kate. I never wrote a love letter in my life."

"Yes," I cried, managing a fairly good giggle. "That's it! A love letter!"

But teasing him like that wasn't a smart thing to do. The words were hardly out of my mouth before he grabbed me roughly by the upper arms. "You keep quiet about this," he threatened, "or you'll be sorry."

When I didn't answer right away, he shook me till I thought my brains were rattling. "I mean it, Kate. You've got to keep quiet."

He looked really desperate. My fingers tightened around the head of the pin, but now it seemed a very ineffectual weapon. "Peter," I begged, my head swimming, "please, let go. You're hurting me."

Peter gave me one last shake. "You'll hurt a lot worse," he said, his expression frightening, "if you don't keep your nose out of this!"

"Yes, Peter." I hated agreeing with him so easily, but it seemed like the expedient thing to do. I would just ask him, very politely, to let me go.

But then, before I could say anything, his hands dropped away from me. "What do you want?" he demanded, looking over my head.

Wondering who had so fortunately chosen that moment to come down the hall past Nell's room, I swung around. And there stood Archie, his cheerful smile a trifle strained.

"Nothing special," Archie said. "Just coming round to see Kate."

Breathing a sigh of relief, I crossed the room to him, surreptitiously returning the pin to my bodice while I pretended to straighten my gown. "Thank you, Peter," I said. "We'll talk again later."

Back in my dressing room, Archie gave me a peculiar look. "What was that all about?"

For some reason — theater loyalty maybe — I didn't want to discuss Peter. Besides, Archie would scold me if he thought I'd been in danger. "Oh, nothing much. We were just talking." I smiled up at Archie and changed the subject. "So what did Betty's mother have to say? Will she convince Wild Willie to tell us what he knows?"

Archie pushed a pile of play books onto the floor and lowered himself onto the chair. "She'd like to help us. She said she'd talked to Willie about it more than once. But he keeps insisting he doesn't know anything."

"It's so exasperating." I sank down on my bench facing him. "Oh, Archie, what are we going to do?"

Running a hand through his hair, Archie looked apologetic. "Don't see what we can do, my dear. I think that we've rather reached a dead end."

I just couldn't accept that. "But Archie, we can't give up. Mrs. Wattly's counting on us. Besides, it's not right! Someone's getting away with murder!"

"I know that," Archie said patiently, "and of course we won't give up. Who knows, maybe Mrs. Wattly will persuade Willie to talk to us."

Archie didn't look like he believed that. And neither did I.

"There must be something we're missing," I went on. "There's got to be a connection between these murders. Some why. Some reason. People don't kill each other without any cause at all."

"I agree," Archie said with that cheery smile of his. "Totally. But I'm afraid that leaves us right back where we began."

"We have to figure it out." I looked at him intently. "I can understand just about anyone wanting to stop Nell's mouth. Permanently." I shrugged. "I mean, after all, she was always yelling — and throwing things. Why, the very day she was killed, I had Betty in my dressing room to fix a cut where Nell had hit her with a pot of makeup. And poor Betty, instead of being upset about the cut, was worried because Nell was yelling at her about some lost paper and —"

I stopped in mid-sentence, staring at him. "Archie! Betty said Nell was dreadfully upset because she couldn't find that paper! Do you suppose it has something to do —"

"A paper?" Archie raised a blond eyebrow. "I don't think so. Betty's mother said she was afraid. Why would Betty be afraid of a piece of paper?"

I leaned forward to grab his arm. "That's what Peter was looking for! It must be it."

"Peter?" Archie's eyebrows went together in puzzlement. "What are you talking about?"

Too late I remembered I hadn't meant to tell on Peter. Now I had to. "Well, earlier, just a little before you came along, I heard someone in the hall and I saw Peter sneak into Nell's dressing room so I followed him. He was looking through her things. I just bet he was after that paper."

Archie sighed and gave me a look that said he was exasperated, but he didn't put any words to his look or scold me. He just ran his hand through his hair, rearranging its general untidiness, and sighed again, more heavily than before.

"Nell was always losing things," I went on, thinking out loud, "putting stuff away and not remembering where she put it." I frowned. "Then she blamed someone else because she couldn't find things."

A strange, almost pained, look crossed Archie's face. He surveyed me thoughtfully for a minute, then got to his feet and crossed the room to pull me up to mine. "Kate, love," he said, looking down into my eyes and taking both my hands in his. "You've no idea how worried I've been. I've had the most horrid day, imagining all the very worst things that could have happened to you. And finding you in that tainted room alone with a man who might be a killer —" He heaved another great sigh. "I'm telling you, Kate, my heart almost leaped clean out of my throat."

"I — I was safe enough," I replied, which wasn't quite the truth, of course. I hadn't felt safe with Peter's big hands on me, but I didn't want Archie to scold me any more.

His frown turned into a half smile. "You're a great trial to me," he said, his voice cheerful again. "And it's such a relief to see you safe and sound that I simply must do this."

He pulled me into his arms, not for a kiss as I had supposed, but for a big hug. "In these few days," he murmured against my hair, "you've become important to me. I don't want anything to hap—" He jerked back. "What the devil!"

In his enthusiasm Archie had hugged me too tight and been stuck with the sharp end of the pin I'd hastily returned to my bodice. He held me off, a rueful look on his face. "What on earth is that thing?"

I laughed and showed him. "It's a brooch, a Celtic brooch that belonged to Mama.

After Nell's murder Papa told me to wear it all the time."

Archie frowned. "Best be careful with it. You could hurt a man."

I couldn't help it — I laughed. "Dear, dear Archie," I said, "that's the general idea. It's for protection."

"Of course." His frown deepened and his expression sobered. "You listen to your father. Make sure you wear it all the time."

"I will, Archie, I promise. Now, did you find out when Robson and Thicket are fighting?"

"Not yet," Archie said, and changed the subject.

CHAPTER EIGHT

Though several days passed in uneventful fashion, I was entirely unable to forget about poor Betty's death, unable to concentrate on my lines. If Nell had been the only victim, well, unkind as it sounds, I might have let the whole matter drop. After all, Nell wasn't much of a loss to the world. Not a good person, not even a good actress. And we did have Bow Street to investigate the crime.

But Betty was different. She had been a good, kindhearted soul, loving her mother, loving Willie. She shouldn't have been killed in that horrid way. Her murderer should be brought to justice.

So all my spare time was eaten up by speculations about the murders. I was convinced that some connection lay between the two. There were plenty of people who might wish to see the end of Nell. I ran some of them through my mind: Lavinia, who had quarreled with Nell, in fact threatened her very life; Peter, whom she'd dismissed so harshly after he claimed she'd promised to marry him; and Lord Foxcroft, who had darkly reminded her that she was his property — bought and paid for. Yes, all of them had some reason to be angry with Nell, but what reason did any of them have to hurt Betty?

There my speculations always came to a halt, because no matter how hard I tried, I could find no reason for anyone to harm Betty. Her murder might have something to do with that mysterious paper, but without the paper itself it was impossible to know.

Finally, exhausted with vague imaginings, I decided to talk to some of the people involved. And so, one day about a week after Nell's death, I made my way to Lavinia's dressing room and rapped on the door.

"Come in," she called.

I had been in her dressing room before. It was the same size and layout as mine and had the same furnishings. It held a dressing table with a mirror above it and a bench before it, one battered wooden chair, a changing screen, and a few pegs on the far wall to hang costumes on. Two people might sit with some comfort in it. Three would be cramped.

Lavinia was alone. She rose from the bench to welcome me. "Kate! Hello. What can I do for you?"

"Oh, nothing." Now that I was there I felt somewhat constrained. After all, I had considered the possibility that she might be the murderer. But since I meant to prove her innocent, surely what I was doing was all right. "I just came to talk a little. I've missed our friendship."

"Come in," she said. "Sit down."

I took the chair she motioned to and she settled back on the bench.

"I'm glad to see you." Her smile, though feeble, was at least a smile. "People seem to be avoiding me lately." She sighed heavily, her dark brows drawing together. "If only I hadn't lost my temper that day. If I hadn't threatened Nell, people wouldn't think I killed her."

"I'm sure they don't all think it," I said swiftly. "I don't. Perhaps it's just that people don't know how to behave. It is an unusual situation."

"Yes," Lavinia agreed, "and very trying, especially with Peter putting the murder on me like he is." She sighed heavily. "I've never done anything to Peter. And for him to accuse me —"

She looked so woebegone that I leaned

forward to pat her arm sympathetically. "He's all cut up, you know. I think he really loved Nell."

Lavinia shook her head. "It's hard to imagine anyone loving her. She was such a —" She paused and looked at me ruefully. "I know it's not proper to speak disrespectfully of the dead."

"You're right," I agreed. "It isn't. But dead or alive, well . . . we both know Nell wasn't a very nice person."

Lavinia smiled. "Indeed we do." Then her smile turned to a frown, her dark brows drawing together again. "But I still can't imagine who would want to kill her."

"She never said anything to you about enemies?"

"To me!" Lavinia cried, raising an eyebrow. "Heavens, no. I wasn't worth being cultivated. Nell always preferred the company of those with money."

I leaned closer. "You mean like Lord Foxcroft?"

Lavinia nodded. "Yes, he was the latest in a long line." A sad wistful look crossed her heavy face. "A strange man — Lord Foxcroft. So autocratic and yet so compelling. If he'd asked me, I would have —" She stopped, laughing a little bitterly. "Yes, in spite of the fact that I love Bob, if Foxcroft had looked in my direction . . . but he wouldn't ask *me.* I ought to despise him, using women as he does."

Bob, I thought. I didn't know Lavinia had a fellow, but I was more interested in Foxcroft. I nodded eagerly. "Isn't it strange? I know just what you mean. He affects me the same way."

Lavinia shook her head, looking even sadder. "Women are sometimes the rankest fools, especially where men are concerned."

"I guess so." I didn't know if I completely understood what she meant. I hadn't yet experienced that kind of dangerous attraction. But the subject of Lord Foxcroft was more fascinating. "Do you suppose he killed her? Lord Foxcroft, I mean?"

Her lips pursed, Lavinia considered my question. Then she shook her head. "I expect he's capable of it. Most of us are, if pushed far enough. But what would he gain? If he didn't want Nell any more, he had only to walk away." She smiled wistfully again. "We both know he'd have no trouble finding a dozen replacements."

I nodded solemnly. She was so right. In fact, I myself — Better not to think of that.

"So, do you think Peter —" I began.

Lavinia's dark brows rose again. "I suppose it's possible — anything's possible —

but I don't think it's likely. Peter's mostly talk and I think he did have some feeling for Nell."

"Well," I went on, "I don't think a thief did it either. I think the same person killed both Betty and Nell." I lowered my voice. "And I think he was after something."

Lavinia's dark eyes widened and she leaned toward me. "After something? Do you know what?"

I opened my mouth to tell her about the lost paper but then reconsidered. Hadn't she just said we were all capable of murder? I took a deep breath. "No, not exactly. But I saw Peter sneak into Nell's dressing room the other day. Couldn't that mean he was looking for something?"

She leaned back. "It could, I suppose. But it doesn't have to. Maybe he just went in there to grieve, to be close to her, you know." Lavinia swallowed hard and sighed. "People do that sometimes."

I nodded. "Yes, I suppose that could be it. And to think I believed Peter was shallow, a man of little heart."

Lavinia shrugged. "I suppose we all have hidden depths."

I thought of that later, back in my dressing room. Could Lavinia be the killer? Was that what she meant about depths? But thinking about that got me nowhere, so eventually I turned to studying my lines for upcoming plays until it was time for rehearsal. This time Peter did better with his lines, but he still kept giving me strange looks that I couldn't figure out. Was he guilty and wondering if I'd guessed it?

Finally Mr. Kemble let us go and I headed back toward my dressing room. I had turned into the passageway, idly wondering why we couldn't have more lights there, when I noticed two figures at the far end in close conversation. They were nothing more than vague dark shapes to me. Just then, one shape disengaged itself and moved away. It looked like the figure of a big man hurrying around the far corner.

So what if it was, I told myself. All sorts of people worked in the theater. It could be a prop man, someone's dresser, a seamstress, any number of people.

The other figure came toward me. Something about the way it moved . . . Lavinia? But why was she coming this way, toward me? Her dressing room was only halfway down the hall, mine was beyond it, almost to the other end and Nell's beyond mine. Lavinia had no reason to walk that far down the hall. Unless. . . .

I walked on, trying to think. Had Lavinia gone to search Nell's room because of what I'd told her earlier? Had she been trying to tell me something, to warn me maybe, when she spoke about anyone being capable of murder? Or was I letting my imagination run wild?

By this time I'd almost reached her door. I did my best to look natural and unconcerned. I was an actress, after all, I should be able to manage that.

Lavinia had left her door open and as I passed she looked up, glancing at me in her mirror. "Oh, Kate, there you are." She swung around and I stopped in her doorway. "I was just down to your dressing room. Thought you'd finished rehearsing."

"Mr. Kemble kept us late." Slowly I let out a sigh of relief. "Did you want something?"

"Not really. I just got lonesome. You going home now?"

I nodded. "Yes, after all that work I need a good supper."

It wasn't till later, in Archie's carriage on the way home, that it came to me. If Lavinia wanted to see me, why hadn't she continued down the hall to meet me? Why had she darted into her dressing room in that furtive fashion? So she'd have time to think up an excuse? Because she didn't want to explain who she was talking to?

Still it was hard for me to suspect Lavinia. Maybe she just hadn't recognized me. The hall was dark. I tried to decide if I should tell Archie about it but he was getting tired of hearing about that lost paper. Furthermore, he was busy telling me about his day.

"And while you were rehearsing," he went on, grinning at me cheerfully, "I popped into Gentleman Jackson's and had myself a few rounds in the ring."

"Rounds in the ring!" That took my attention off the murders. "You could get hurt doing that."

Archie looked affronted. "Really, Kate! I'll have you know that for an amateur, I'm quite a good boxer. Gentleman Jackson says so himself."

"But Archie —"

"If you want me to discover the whereabouts of the Robson-Thicket fight, I've got to be where they talk boxing." He gave me a rather devilish grin. "And besides, if you persist in getting into the suds, then it might come in handy to know how to defend you."

That made sense, of course, but I didn't mean to let him have the last word. "Very well, but I still don't like the idea."

His grin widened. "Why, Kate my love, are you afraid someone will land me a facer and ruin my good looks?"

"What good looks?" I retorted. But he was nearer the truth than I cared to admit. I didn't want him to get hurt.

CHAPTER NINE

Two days later, Archie came into my dressing room after rehearsal. "Well, that settles it," he said firmly. "You can't possibly go to the Robson-Thicket fight."

"And why not?" I demanded, already bristling as I turned from my dressing table to face him.

"Because it's clear out at Hungerford, that's why." Archie's face took on the stubborn look I was beginning to know. "And it's tomorrow morning. Since boxing matches have been declared illegal, they're being held outside the city now. And they only let the name of the place out a day or so before the fight, hoping the local magistrates won't hear about it in time to stop it." He shook his head and tried to look disappointed, but I could hear the relief in his voice. "Hungerford's too far. You can't possibly go."

"Yes, I can," I said stubbornly. "And I will."

Poor Archie. His face turned several shades of red and he ran his fingers through his untidy blond hair in a distracted way. "Kate, I beg of you. How can you think of such a thing? The fellows always go out to the place the day before. All the inns around will be packed. If I take you among them, your reputation —"

I laughed. "Dear Archie, I'm an actress, remember! What reputation do I have to lose?"

Archie sighed. "But you turned down my offer and —"

I leaned forward to put a hand on his arm. "Archie, I turned down your offer on principle — principle, understand — because I am my own person, because I just won't be owned by anyone."

He looked relieved and I realized he'd thought I had an aversion to his person. That wasn't true, of course. It really *was* a matter of principle. But this was not the time to think of that. I had to find out who had killed Betty. Was I going to learn that at the fight? I didn't know.

I regarded Archie soberly. "It's simply no use your putting me off about this fight. I mean to go to it with or without you. Now, do you mean to let me go out there alone?"

I admit it was rather cruel of me to force Archie into doing what I wanted by playing on his feelings for me. But I couldn't get over the idea that the exchange of wary glances between Willie and Bob at mention of this fight meant something or that the fight was in some way connected to Betty's murder. And how could I learn anything if I couldn't even get there?

Archie gazed at me in exasperation. "Kate, either we shall have to travel all night, or we shall have to stay at an inn. At big bouts like this, every room is filled from wall to wall. Are you prepared for that?"

I swallowed. I wasn't all that sure of my disguise on close inspection. And I certainly had no desire to spend the night surrounded by strange males in various stages of undress.

"You have a closed carriage," I pointed out. "I know. I've ridden in it more than once."

Archie looked more unhappy.

"If we leave after the show," I explained in my sweetest and most reasonable tones, "we can get there by morning, see the fight, and be back in time for the next evening's performance."

Archie groaned. "You expect me to spend

the night with you in a closed carriage and not —"

"Of course," I replied. "I expect you to be a gentleman."

"I'm a crazy gentleman," Archie said grimly, his moustache quivering. "I must be, or by now I'd have found someone else to —"

"You may do that," I said sweetly. "Anytime you like. I just hope you and I can remain friends." I leaned toward him. "I'm fond of your company, Archie, and very good company it is. I'd be most sorry to lose your friendship."

Archie shook his head. "I cannot believe this. You expect me —" Suddenly his face lightened. "Your father!" he cried in such obvious relief that I almost laughed. "He'll never allow you to do this."

"And that is precisely why we won't tell him." I leaned closer. "Will we?"

Archie groaned again, louder. "He's going to kill me."

"Oh, Archie, you worry too much." I stood up. "Now, let's see. You can help me decide how to dress."

In the end, I wore the same clothes I'd worn to the Cock and Bull. When I was tucking my red curls under a boy's cap, I considered wearing a wig. I could easily borrow one from the prop room but I decided against it. A wig would just complicate matters, mean one more thing to worry about. Anyways, no one was going to recognize I was a woman. They'd all be busy watching the fight.

After the performance was over, I changed into the male clothes and, wrapping my cloak around me, hurried out to where Archie waited in his closed carriage.

When he saw me coming, he opened the door from the inside. In the dim glow of the carriage lamps his face looked pale. "Really, Kate, I don't think —"

I climbed in and settled beside him. "Please, Archie, there's no point in arguing with me. Let's just go."

Heaving a huge sigh, Archie leaned across me to pull the door shut. Then he gave me a rueful look and said in an aggrieved imitation of me in my role of Sir Harry. "An honourable Lover is the greatest Slave in Nature."

"Archie! Where did you hear that?"

"I was watching rehearsals and the line stuck in my mind. Quite an appropriate line." He grinned. "Farquhar must have known a woman like you."

I bristled just a little. "I don't know why

you say that," I insisted. "Anyhow, the line doesn't apply to us. You're not my lover and —"

"Only because you won't let me be."

Ignoring that, I went on. "And you're certainly not my slave."

Archie laughed. "That's what you think. Look at me. I'm going to be shut up in this carriage with you all night! In spite of your boy's clothes, you're beautiful and fetching." He groaned. "And me forbidden to so much as *kiss* you."

I cleared my throat and looked demurely down at my folded hands. "Ah, Archie, ah, I don't seem to remember forbidding kissing. But if you don't care to —"

Archie didn't wait any longer. He pulled me into his arms and kissed me quite thoroughly.

When I could breathe again, I disentangled myself, but only a little, and said, "Please, Archie, remember, we have all night."

We arrived in Hungerford shortly after dawn. By then Archie had kissed himself out and I had fallen asleep against his very comfortable shoulder. He woke me in the morning, a beautiful May morning with the sun shining and the larks singing. He had the coachman pull off the road so we could make our morning toilet in a secluded grove of trees. Then we got back in the coach and Archie set forth the provisions he'd thoughtfully provided.

"You're a prince," I said around a mouthful of bun and boiled egg.

"And you are the most beautiful, exciting woman in the world." Archie smiled hugely. In spite of his sleepless night he was looking exceedingly chipper — the effect of those kisses, perhaps. I hoped I hadn't given him the wrong impression. I'd enjoyed his kisses very much, but I still had no intention of going into keeping.

"Do I look the part?" I asked, pulling a little anxiously at my jacket.

Archie leaned over to brush a crumb off my chin. "I suppose you'll do," he said grudgingly. "But how anyone can think you're a man with that adorable little face and —"

I patted his arm. "Archie love, I believe you're just a trifle biased."

"Not me." His grin made me want to kiss him again.

His compliments were beginning to make me feel warm but not as warm as his kisses had. Fortunately he didn't notice because he'd chosen that moment to look out at the countryside. "People are on their way already." He banged on the ceiling and called up to the driver, "Follow those carriages."

By the time we reached the site of the match, a crowd was gathering. I gazed around in amazement. It was like we were going to some great fair or celebration. Carriages were coming in from all directions, some flying banners, some even carrying musicians and their instruments. Martial music and the sound of hundreds of excited voices filled the air.

Country people pushed through hedges and jumped ditches, swarming nearer. The grass was still wet with dew and the ground was already getting trampled into mud, all except the spot reserved for the ring. No one dared to tread there.

Aristocrats and farmers, hostlers and tutors, men of all walks of life, stood shoulder to shoulder, crowded ever closer. Archie managed, I'm not sure how, to get us close to the ring, too. I'd never been so crammed among people. I stayed close to Archie, as close as I could get, while all around us rose a great babble of voices.

A ripple of anticipation raced through the crowd, half cheer, half sigh, and a path opened through its midst. "Thicket's coming," Archie said.

And here Thicket came. On one side marched his second, on the other his bottle holder. Thicket himself was wrapped in a great loose robe. He was a big man, bigger than Wild Man Willie, and it looked like his knock-knees might give way under his great weight. But he smiled at the crowd and it cheered as he threw his hat into the ring and began to take off his robe.

The crowd parted on the other side and Robson came strutting along, sucking loudly on an orange. When he reached the ring, he tossed the orange rind away, not even looking where it fell or who it might hit. His lip curling contemptuously, Robson looked Thicket up and down, before he, too, began to strip to his fighting clothes.

They were such a contrast. Thicket was big everywhere with a ponderous look about him while Robson was almost lean, and moved lightly, with a cat-like agility.

They tossed up to see who would face the sun. Thicket would have it in his eyes. Then they were led up to the scratch, shook hands, and went at it.

I knew boxing was a violent sport, and I had expected to be sickened, or at least dismayed, by seeing two men pound on each other. But Robson had showed so cocky, so arrogant, that I wanted to see him go down. He flew at Thicket, throwing one blow after another, but Thicket just stood there, taking them, clenching his teeth and squinting against the sun. The man was a rock. How could he endure so many blows?

Finally the round was over. Half a minute, thirty short seconds, was all the rest they got between rounds. It seemed inhuman.

In the excitement I'd almost forgotten my reason for being there. But while the fighters were resting, I remembered.

"Think this one's a cross?" I asked, loud enough for those around us to hear.

Archie sent me a look of dismay. "No," he said shortly, "it's not fixed."

A rough looking fellow on my left laughed boisterously. "Better listen to the lad," he said to Archie. "Probably 'tis a cross. Last time Robson fought — that'un was a cross fer sure."

I turned to him eagerly. "Tell me. How do you know?"

He grinned, showing the stumps of several discolored teeth. "Don't need to know," he said. "Word gets 'round. Word's usually right."

I wanted to press the man for details, but the next round had begun and he turned back to the fighters.

It wasn't a pretty sight — Thicket stand-ing there, taking blow after blow. He landed a few himself, and they were fairly good blows, too, but Robson kept dancing around the ring, smirking until I'd like to have lent him a facer myself.

One minute Thicket was taking the blows, stolidly, hardly moving, and the next his left arm shot out, catching Robson on the eye and cheekbone. The crowd roared in tri-umph as Robson staggered.

But he rallied and flailed back. The fight went on, round after round. After a while I began to feel pity for them both. Their faces were each a mass of bloodied bruises. Rob-son had his eyes swollen half shut, Thicket a split lip, but they still fought on. The sight of so much blood was beginning to sicken me, and when Thicket struck Robson an-other sharp blow and blood spurted from his nose, my stomach rebelled. The food that had seemed so welcome a few hours earlier set up a mad battle.

I clutched at Archie's arm. "Sick," I mouthed. In the uproar it was impossible to make him hear me. "Sick," I repeated, covering my mouth with my hand. "Going to be sick."

I don't know if it was my expression or my lack of color, but in the very act of brushing my other hand off his sleeve, Archie stopped and hustled me through the crowd to a place where I could be, and was, thoroughly sick.

We were still there when a great roar went up from behind us. "Hell and damnation!" Archie cried. "We've missed the end of it!" And he started back for the ring as fast as he could go.

"Archie! Wait!" I don't know if I was more scared of being left alone or of not knowing the outcome of the fight. At any rate, I hurried after him as fast as my weak knees would carry me.

Archie pushed his way back toward the ring, all the while muttering. "What happened? Did you see what happened?"

"Aye, mate." It was our friend of the discolored teeth. "Thicket took 'im." He flashed me a stumpy smile. "Looks to me like the lad had the right of it. Another cross, it is."

I grabbed his dirty sleeve. "Please, tell me, how do you know?"

Archie was pulling at my other arm, trying to drag me away, but I dug in my heels, refusing to be budged. "Please," I repeated. "Tell me."

A burly looking farmer pushed closer to us. "Who says 'tis a cross? 'Tis a dirty lie!

Ned Thicket never done such a thing."

"Oh yeah?" Stumpy cried. "I say 'twas a cross. And they was both in on't."

The farmer shoved his ruddy face almost into Stumpy's. "Yer wrong. Dead wrong." And he accompanied his statement with a raised fist the size of a ham. "Thicket's true blue."

I tried to back away, but the crowd behind me pressed forward, eager for more bloodshed.

Stumpy stood his ground, raising his own grubby fist. "I say 'twas a cross. And it —"

The rest of the sentence never got out of his mouth. The farmer dealt him a sharp blow. Stumpy hit him back, and in seconds the whole crowd had gone berserk, yelling and punching each other.

I had a very little idea of the art of manly self-defense, but I put up my fists, prepared to do my best. And that's when Archie clipped me neatly on the jaw and the world went black.

I woke up inside the carriage where I was given to understand that I had made an awful hatch of things, and precipitated a near riot, proof of which Archie offered by telling me to look out the carriage window.

The pandemonium out there was incredible. All kinds of men surged around the carriage trading blows. Some fell and just lay there. Others fought awhile, then put their arms around each other, and sauntered off together while others battled on.

"Get us out of here!" Archie called up to the driver. "Now!"

The ride back to London was less than pleasant. Archie spent much of the time telling me how foolish I'd been and the rest sitting in aggrieved silence. I couldn't blame him. Because of me he'd missed the end of the fight.

I had to concede that he had a point. If the fight had been fixed, the people responsible were hardly going to stand around discussing it.

Gingerly I touched my tender chin. He hadn't even apologized for hitting me. Hardly the act of a gentleman. I considered telling him so, but he looked so grim that I decided I'd better keep silent.

I sat in silence, too, until we reached the theater. Still wearing that injured expression, Archie reached across me to open the door.

Instead of getting out, I leaned closer to him. "Archie, I want to say thank you."

He gave me a look that would have wilted a lesser woman and didn't do me any good.

I tried again. "Perhaps I was just a little —"

Archie snorted. "A little! Kate, you behaved abominably, putting us both in danger!"

"Yes, well, I didn't mean to." I put my hand on his sleeve. "And I'm truly sorry."

He pulled his arm away. "Better get out, Kate. The play'll be starting soon."

He was right. I had to get inside. But something in his face told me I might have gone too far, and at that moment I knew, quite definitely, that I didn't want to lose him. "Archie, I —"

"Goodbye, Kate," he said grimly.

CHAPTER TEN

After Archie left me, I stood staring at his departing carriage in disbelief. Finally I realized he wasn't going to turn around, and I stumbled into the theater. I could hardly believe he'd actually left, but I couldn't stop to worry about it then — the play had to go on.

After the performance was over, I went home in a hired carriage with Mama and Papa. It felt strange not to have Archie waiting for me. In a short time he'd become an important part of my life. I still didn't want him for a protector, but his kisses had been very nice, well, actually better than nice.

I was very much afraid that I was going to miss Archie dreadfully if he really meant goodbye. He was such a comfortable person to be with — probably because of those three younger sisters of his which he called "precocious brats," but with an underlying warmth that held brotherly affection.

When we reached home, I was still thinking about those kisses. Had Archie meant that last goodbye to be forever or was he just trying to scare me? Papa opened the door to our rooms and turned to me. "Kate, I must speak with you."

Of course, I'd known it was inevitable. How could Papa not notice that I hadn't come home the night before? But in my worry over Archie's pique, I'd pushed Papa's imminent lecture clean out of my thoughts.

While Mama lit the lamp, I took a chair and waited. Papa loomed in front of me, wearing his "how-can-you-do-this-to-me?" look. I'd seen it before, of course, but I'd rather not have faced it that night. I hadn't felt so low in a very long time. I'd learned nothing at the boxing match and I'd made Archie so angry he might stop seeing me. Now Papa was going to read me a royal scold. How much more did I have to endure?

Papa cleared his throat and said in his most tragic tones, "Kate, you didn't come home last night."

"Yes, Papa," I said meekly. Meekness was usually the best approach.

He gave me a stern look. "Did you — did you —" He stammered to a halt and for a moment I thought embarrassment might make him give up the whole lecture. But Papa was made of sterner stuff. He took a deep breath and bellowed out, "Did you spend the night with Viscount Barrington?"

"Yes, Papa, but not as you think. We didn't —"

Papa turned scarlet. "Catherine Louise Ketterling! Your mama and I raised you to be a decent woman. How could you do this? You —"

"Papa." I had to interrupt before he could get carried away by his own rhetoric, otherwise we'd never get to bed. "It wasn't what you think. We just went to Hungerford to the Thicket-Robson fight."

Papa sat down abruptly. "You went to a boxing match?"

"Yes, Papa. That's why I didn't come home. We had to drive all night, you see, and —"

"Why?" Papa asked in puzzlement. "Why did you go to a boxing match?"

And right then the thought popped into my head — so beautiful, so apt. I'd never known I could be so devious. "Why, Papa, to study for my role as Sir Harry, of course. I wanted to see how to behave on such occasions."

From the corner of my eye, I caught

Mama's skeptical expression. But she kept silent — she wouldn't give me away.

My pronouncement had rendered Papa temporarily speechless, so I hurried on, trying to secure my position. "You always tell me to study for my parts. To try to discover why people behave as they do." I leaned forward eagerly. "It was so exciting, Papa. So many people to watch! And the fight itself —"

He was weakening. I could see it in his expression. "But a fight, a woman at a —"

"Oh, I didn't go as a woman."

He looked bewildered.

"I wore my breeches and cap, Papa. Everyone thought I was a lad. And I stayed close to Archie." I didn't think it necessary or wise to tell Papa about the near riot I'd caused or the kisses Archie and I had shared during the long night together.

Papa shook his head and gazed at me mournfully for several minutes. Then he heaved himself wearily to his feet, "I think I understand. But don't worry us like this again, Kate. Let us know where you're going."

"Yes, Papa, I will. And wait till you see the swagger I learned. It adds a great deal to Sir Harry."

Papa nodded and took himself off to bed.

After a hug and a whispered, "Be careful," Mama followed him.

I went to my bed, too, but not to sleep. Long into the night, I lay awake, puzzling over what I knew and didn't know. And wondering if I'd ever see Archie again.

Before I fell asleep, I remembered Archie saying that since his brother's death the year before, he managed the estate where his mother and sisters resided. Would he leave for the country without seeing me again?

The next day was even worse. Everywhere I went, I expected to see Archie's cheery smile, hear his warm chuckle but of course he wasn't there.

Toward midafternoon, Peter and I finished running over our lines for the coming play. The boy who carried messages told me Mr. Kemble wanted to see me in his office.

At my knock on the open door, Mr. Kemble looked up from the papers on his desk. "Come in, Kate."

While he surveyed me solemnly, I waited for him to reprimand me for missing rehearsal the day before. I'd already decided to give him the same excuse I'd given Papa. It had worked really well on Papa. So maybe . . .

"These murders are most unfortunate,"

Mr. Kemble said, his voice even deeper than usual. "However, business doesn't seem to have suffered."

"That's good." I understood that Mr. Kemble had to think about the theater. All our livelihoods depended on it. Was it possible he wasn't going to mention my lapse? I waited, trying my best to look humble and attentive.

He drummed on the top of his desk with his fingertips. "You've been a good trouper, Kate."

"I try, sir." I heard it in his voice. I wasn't going to get away free. It was coming now.

He frowned. "Yesterday you were missing from rehearsal."

"Yes, sir." Suddenly my excuse didn't look so sound. Not at all.

"You know, of course, that rehearsals are necessary."

I felt about two years old. "Yes, sir." I decided to use my excuse after all. It might work — and it was all I had. "You see, sir, I got a chance to go to the Thicket-Robson fight." His heavy eyebrows went up and I hurried on. "I wanted to observe how men behave at a boxing match. I thought perhaps my portrayal of Sir Harry was a trifle too feminine." I bowed my head abjectly. "I thought I could learn something to improve

Sir Harry, you see."

Mr. Kemble stared at me while the seconds ticked by. Would he believe me? Finally he sighed. "Very well, Kate. But I'd suggest that future trips be taken in your free time, not when you should be here working."

"Oh yes, sir!" I cried. "I won't miss, sir, not any more. I promise. And thank you for being so understanding. I think —"

He sighed. "That's all Kate." And he waved me out.

I played Sir Harry that night, resplendent in my green satin breeches. Peter got through his lines without any breakdown, and I did such an excellent job with mine that the audience loved me. The pit was packed, the boxes too. I bowed toward the spectators and in that moment I could have sworn I saw Willie and Bruising Bob in the pit, but the audience was roaring its approval, and I had to glance around the whole place again, smiling at them all. When I looked back, I couldn't see either fighter. Maybe I'd just imagined seeing them because I'd been thinking so much about Betty.

Every actress knows how the approbation of the crowd can warm the soul. It did that for me that night. But still my triumph seemed hollow. I didn't seem to care how many people approved my performance. The one who mattered wasn't there to see me. Archie's goodbye had been real.

Though I didn't feel like it, I changed into my best gown and went to the greenroom as usual. Being available to patrons was part of an actress's duty. And Mr. Kemble wasn't too happy with me already.

I stood there, the center of much attention, hearing compliment after compliment, and not really caring. For one thing, Peter hovered near me with a proprietary air that nearly drove me to distraction. Whatever else I might be, I would never be *his*. So between easing out from under his sweaty hand and acknowledging compliments, it was hard not to call it quits. Still, the prospect of going back to my dressing room alone wasn't much better, so I stood there nodding and trying to smile, wishing for some of Archie's cheery chatter.

"Where's your admirer?" I hadn't see him come up behind me, but I recognized Lord Foxcroft's voice. I turned and he was looking at me!

"He's not in attendance tonight?" he asked, completely ignoring Peter who still stood beside me.

"No. We — He — No." It was just like Lavinia had said. Foxcroft exuded a dangerous magnetism, an aura of power, that was particularly fascinating to a woman.

He took a step closer. "My congratulations. You do Sir Harry well."

"Thank you. I enjoy it." Could he have remembered seeing me in the Cock and Bull? But his eyes showed only admiration.

"I could see that." Foxcroft let his gaze slide down to the top of my gown and the small amount of flesh that showed above it. Like a green girl, I flushed.

"Still," he said, reaching out to finger my hair, "though you make an admirable rake, you make an even more exciting woman."

Invitation warmed his eyes and for a few seconds I almost forgot my cherished principle of independence. Almost but not quite. I managed a small laugh. "You flatter me, milord."

Through this whole exchange, Peter stood glowering. He moved a step closer to me. "Kate, I —"

Foxcroft cleared his throat, that was all, just cleared his throat. But Peter went silent.

"Thank you for a pleasurable evening," Foxcroft said, bending low over my fingers. "I trust you'll give me many, many more."

His eyes and his tone implied a different pleasure than that of watching a play, but I merely nodded, pretending not to understand, and said, "I enjoy the theater."

His slow sure smile said as plain as words that he knew that I knew what he meant, and that if he wanted me, he would have me. And then he moved away. I saw the way others returned his smile, mesmerized, hoping against hope, each of them, to become his new mistress. I understood.

I tried not to do it, but I couldn't keep my gaze from following him. That's how I know that Peter didn't say a word the whole time Foxcroft was in the room, but the minute Foxcroft was out the door, Peter turned to me, "Kate, you mustn't do it. You simply mustn't do it!"

I'm an actress, so I feigned ignorance. "Do what, Peter?"

Peter scowled and grabbed my arm. "I saw the way he looked at you! But you mustn't do it."

"Why, Peter? Why not?"

He looked away from me. "You just mustn't."

For a few minutes I considered letting Peter go on thinking that I might take Foxcroft as my protector. Then I remembered how Peter liked to talk. And I didn't want people to hear that about me. Especially I didn't want Archie to hear it.

So I took a deep breath and stared Peter

full in the face. "There's no need to worry about me! I'm not interested in what Lord Foxcroft can offer me." That wasn't precisely true. His physical presence was very attractive to me, but I didn't care for the price I'd have to pay. "I am not interested," I repeated to Peter. "Not at all."

And Peter heaved a huge sigh and said, "Thank God!"

CHAPTER ELEVEN

The days passed. Unfortunately none of them brought me any closer to solving the murders, and my usual joy in performing was in danger of being lost. Still I rehearsed, playing my parts to the best of my ability. As long as I breathed I would do that.

About a week after Archie had told me that cold good-bye, I showed up for rehearsal at the usual time. The minute I walked in the door Peter pounced on me. "Have you heard?" he asked, putting a wet hand on my arm.

"Heard what?" Easing away, I tried to curb my annoyance. I felt sorry for Peter, but not that sorry.

"They've arrested her," he said, watching me closely.

My heart turned over. "Arrested who?"

"Lavinia, of course. They say she's the one who killed Nell."

"Lavinia? Why?"

"Jealousy," Peter said, his eyes bright. "She knew Nell was a better actress."

Poor Peter. Love had made him so blind. Still, I knew better than to argue with him. "But what about Betty? Why should Lavinia kill Betty?"

Peter's gaze shifted away from me and his eyes were uneasy. "A cracksman killed Betty, a thief she caught robbing Nell."

"Poppycock!" I still didn't see how anyone could believe that. "Two murders in the same room, committed in the same way, and by two entirely different people? Unconnected? I don't believe it."

Peter shrugged. "You don't have to believe it. But the magistrate obviously does. Lavinia's going to be tried for Nell's murder."

I still didn't understand. "But why now? Why didn't they arrest her before?"

"I'm not privy to the magistrate's reasoning," Peter made a face. "I suppose someone insisted Lavinia be arrested and brought to trial."

I could hardly bear to think of it. Lavinia was such a kindhearted soul. I simply couldn't believe she'd killed Betty. Maybe with provocation she might have killed Nell. But Betty? I just couldn't believe that. If only I hadn't been so foolish and made Archie angry with me, I could ask him to help Lavinia.

Well, I'd wanted a good reason to approach him, though not this one, and it looked like that's what I'd have to do. I'd have to ask Archie for help. And if he refused. . . .

"Mr. Kemble wants to see you," Peter said in that badgering tone of his. "He said as soon as you come in you're to go to his office."

"All right, all right. I'm going."

I made my way to Mr. Kemble's office, wondering what else could possibly be wrong. The door was open as usual. "Mr. Kemble? You wanted to see me?"

He looked up from behind his battered desk. "Yes, Kate. I suppose you heard the news."

"Yes, sir. Poor Lavinia. But I can't believe she killed anyone."

"I can't speak to that," Mr. Kemble went on. "Though I'm very sorry for Lavinia's troubles. This is a most unfortunate occurrence all around."

"Yes, sir."

"Most unfortunate for the theater."

And then I realized what he meant. With Mrs. Siddons's baby almost due, Nell dead, and Lavinia in prison, there was no one to play Desdemona to his Othello. "Maybe we can do *The Constant Couple* some more, sir, or —" Mr. Kemble's frown stopped me in mid-sentence.

He looked almost ferocious. "No, Kate. We have advertised *Othello* and *Othello* is what we'll do."

With a sinking feeling, I ran over in my mind the actresses remaining in the company. "But, sir, there's no one —"

"Your father assures me that you have played the role many times."

My stomach fell into my boots. "But —"

"He tells me that you're more than adequate for the part." Mr. Kemble frowned, his heavy brows drawing together in a way that meant he wasn't to be argued with. "In the circumstances that's all we can ask."

"But —"

"That's all, Kate. Start brushing up on your lines." And he waved me out and went back to his papers.

But I didn't go. Oh, Papa! If he'd been in earshot then, I'd have scorched his ears! I was no Desdemona.

But . . . there might be one advantage to playing the part. "Mr. Kemble, sir?"

He looked up, his eyebrows growing together again. "Yes?"

"Could I — could I have Nell's dressing room, please?"

He was so surprised he forgot to frown at me.

"It's — it's bigger." I hastened to give the first excuse I could think of, though I didn't know if it was true.

I could almost see him thinking another temperamental actress but I didn't care. If I had to act Desdemona, I was going to at least get a chance to examine Nell's things, to look for that illusive piece of paper, or any other clue that might be there.

He sighed. "I don't see why not." He eyed me critically. "Better get your mother to alter Nell's costumes for you. They'll be too long the way they are. Have her fix them all."

I nodded, not at all happy at the prospect of playing that tragic heroine. But at least Mrs. Wattly would have more work for her needle. Archie might want to abandon me, but I was sure he wouldn't forsake the poor woman in that barren little room.

Well, I thought, making my way to my dressing room, I needed Brinson to deliver the costumes to Mrs. Wattly, so there was another reason for seeking an interview with Archie. But would he see me?

That very hour I tried to compose a note to Archie. I found it so difficult to make it sound right that finally I gave up in despair and simply wrote, "Archie, Lavinia's been arrested for Nell's murder. Please help."

I dispatched the note by one of the boys who ran errands and went back to rehearsal.

The long afternoon passed with no reply from Archie. I tried to resign myself to the fact that he had truly meant that chilly goodbye and had possibly even left the city.

Considering the nervous condition I was in, it was fortunate my part that evening was a minor one. What time I wasn't on stage, I spent peering out from the wings. But Archie wasn't in his box. He hadn't been there all week and apparently he wasn't going to be there tonight. He wasn't going to answer my plea for help. He was still angry at me — maybe forever.

When they started the afterpiece, a farce that I had no role in, I turned wearily toward the dressing rooms, glad the evening was over.

As usual the passageway was dim and poorly lit, but I was feeling too despondent to care. I couldn't believe how much I missed Archie. He'd been so kind to me and I had used him dreadfully. I missed his cheery smile, his blond good looks and that twinkle in his clear gray eyes.

I was almost to my dressing room door when I heard a noise — a noise in my dressing room! Before I knew it, I had Mama's brooch clutched in my hand and was pushing the door open. A man stood in the shadows by the changing screen, his back to me.

I raised my brooch/pin, ready to . . .

He turned. "My God, Kate!" Archie yelled. "It's me!"

"A-Archie! Oh, Archie!" I lowered the hand that held the pin and leaned back weakly against the wall, my body all a-tremble.

Two quick steps and he pulled me into his arms. "Here now, Kate. Easy, girl. You sent for me, you know. Didn't you expect me to come?"

Crushed against his chest, I fought back the stupid tears. "Yes, but, but, I didn't see you out front. And so I thought —"

"I knew you didn't have much of a part tonight, so I came back here to wait."

He put me from him and tenderly wiped a tear from my cheek. "Sit down, love," he said. "Now tell me why your friend has been arrested. I thought the magistrate didn't have enough evidence."

I sank down on my bench and Archie pulled the chair close. "I thought so, too," I said. "Now they're saying she killed Nell. Archie, I just can't believe it. And I know she didn't kill Betty. I just know it."

Archie nodded sympathetically. "I understand."

How like him to know exactly what I was talking about. "Oh, Archie, I've missed you dreadfully. I'm awfully sorry about the way I behaved at the fight. Will you forgive me?"

Archie looked a little sheepish. "Yes, Kate. And I guess I owe you an apology, too." He sighed and ran a hand through his hair. "You see, you are driving me to distraction, and that riot you started at the fight —"

He shuddered. "Having to knock you out like that! Upon my word, I've never struck a woman in my life, but I thought you were going to get hurt. Then when you gave me such a good opportunity to be angry, well, I decided I'd just take advantage of it — get over you, you see."

He made a wry face. "But it didn't work." He leaned forward and took my hands in his. "I just couldn't get you out of my mind." He sighed heavily. "The truth is, Kate, my darling girl, I have no sense where you're concerned, no sense whatsoever."

"Oh, Archie, I'm so glad! That is," I stammered on, falling into confusion at the thought that he might misunderstand me, "I'm glad we're friends again."

Archie nodded. "I could wish for something more than friendship from you, but I'm a patient man. I can wait."

Somehow in that short week we'd been apart Archie seemed to have grown older. And I felt younger, almost embarrassed, not knowing how to reply to him.

Then I remembered that Archie didn't know what Mr. Kemble had told me. "Archie, guess what! I'm to play Desdemona —"

"Desdemona?" To his credit Archie tried not to look startled, but the squeak of surprise in his voice gave him away.

I grinned. "I know. Isn't it awful? It wasn't my idea. Mr. Kemble insisted. And since I have to do it, I asked him if I could have Nell's dressing room."

Archie's eyebrows rose drastically. "What on earth for?"

"So we can search it, of course. For the paper."

Archie shook his head. "The paper that isn't there. Mad," he went on in tragic tones, though his gray eyes were sparkling,

"I am stark raving mad to have returned to this!"

CHAPTER TWELVE

Early the next morning Archie dropped me at the theater. While I packed Nell's personal belongings and set them aside, he went off to check on Lavinia's situation. Packing took some time, because I examined each item very carefully, even to turning over perfume bottles and looking inside powder boxes, but all to no avail. I didn't find any papers. I also packed up Nell's costumes and sent them off to Mrs. Wattly by Brinson.

Then I started on my things. Moving me was simple enough. Since all the rooms were laid out and furnished the same way, I just carried things from my old room and put them in the same place in my new one.

Around noon I set the last pots of makeup in place and went to the dusty window to look out on Floral Street. It wasn't so bad being in the room when I was busy, but now that I had nothing left to do, I kept thinking about Betty and Nell, lying there on the floor. So dead.

When I heard footsteps in the hall, I swung around quickly. To my relief it was Archie.

"All done?" he asked cheerfully.

"Yes, it didn't take long. What did the magistrate say?"

Archie's smile vanished. "Very little. Said he couldn't do a thing. That his superiors insisted on Lavinia's arrest. I couldn't get any more than that out of him." He looked around. "How about you? Any luck?"

I shook my head. "No. And I looked *everywhere.* I don't understand it, I thought for sure the paper would be here."

"The paper," Archie repeated, sinking down on the chair that hadn't yet had time to accumulate any mess. "I think that paper has long since disappeared. We're wasting our time looking for it."

I crossed to the bench and sat down, too. I was inclined to agree with him, but there seemed to be no other clue. Perhaps if we had the paper we still wouldn't know any more, but it kept nagging at me. I couldn't get over the feeling that that paper was important.

Archie and I ate a meal that Brinson brought us — bread and cheese, apples and tea. Then it was time for rehearsal. I didn't want to rehearse Desdemona; I didn't want to play Desdemona. What a sorry performance it was going to be. Not just because of me, either. The actress who was playing Emilia had never had a speaking part of more than two lines before this. She'd be stumbling over every other word. Probably I'd have to feed her half her lines. Even the great Mr. Kemble wouldn't be able to carry this off.

"Archie," I said, "why don't you go? Just get out of here. I don't have any part in this evening's production." I smiled. "So that's what I mean to do as soon as rehearsal's over — go home."

Archie glanced around the dressing room, a look of distaste on his face. "I don't like it," he said. "I don't like your being in here. This room gives me the trembles."

I wasn't too fond of it myself, especially now that we hadn't found the paper, or anything else that might help, but I wasn't about to say so. After all, the move had been my idea. "I'm going to be rehearsing all afternoon," I pointed out. "You don't want to see this rehearsal. Really, Archie, you don't." I rubbed my forehead where a headache was starting already. "It embarrasses me just to think of it. On my own I wouldn't do it. I know better than to play Desdemona, but Mr. Kemble insists and —"

Archie hitched his chair closer, took my hand in his and patted it. "You'll do quite well, my dear. You're a trouper." He got up, still holding my hand, and smiled down at me. "But if you want me to go, I will." He kissed my hand and released it.

Impulsively, I jumped to my feet and hugged him.

When I stepped back, he gave me a startled look.

Embarrassed by the memory of his kisses, actually our kisses, I hurried on. "You know very well that I shall make the most miserable Desdemona ever seen."

Archie's cheeks turned slowly pink. He was not an accomplished liar. "Now, Kate, I —"

"It's all right," I interrupted, "I know my limitations. You go on. Let me make a fool of myself without you watching."

Archie kissed me lightly on the lips, a familiarity brought on no doubt by my hugging him, or perhaps he was thinking of our night in his carriage. At any rate, I didn't protest. "I'll send Brinson tomorrow to pick up those costumes from Mrs. Wattly," Archie said. "She'll have to work fast to have them ready in time."

"I know but she doesn't have to do them all right away." I couldn't keep from sighing. "I don't see why Mr. Kemble has to do the play as scheduled. I just don't see."

Archie walked me to the stage where I told him good-bye. Then I spent the next hours trying to think like Desdemona. Mr. Kemble frowned and sighed, but I didn't need that to know I wasn't doing well. "Kate, Kate," he said. "Desdemona stands in awe of Othello. She's quite taken by his heroic tales — and the man himself. You might say she even worships him."

I nodded earnestly, but try as I might I couldn't imagine such awe.

"Can't you play it as my sister does?" Mr. Kemble asked, obviously already knowing the answer. "You've watched her many times."

"I'm trying, sir." But Mrs. Siddons was a proper tragedienne, and I was a hoyden pressed into playing a part that wasn't right for me — would *never* be right for me. Then I was thinking of Papa's repeated words of advice and I knew I needed the motive, the *why. Why* would a man inspire such feelings in a woman?

I tried to think. Money? Title? Power? All

three? And that led me to Lord Foxcroft, and the memory of the conversation Lavinia and I had had about how women were sometimes the rankest fools where men were concerned.

Haughty Lord Foxcroft made me feel rather helpless, quite unlike my usual confident self, honored to have him deign to *look* at me. So that's the way I played it, picturing him as Othello, remembering the breathless feeling I got when Foxcroft stopped to talk to me after *The Constant Couple,* remembering how the heat in his eyes thrilled me even while it frightened me, remembering that when *he* paid attention to me I felt special, and, God forgive me, even grateful.

Mr. Kemble stopped heaving those giant sighs. When the rehearsal was over, he actually smiled at me. "Excellent work, Kate. Excellent."

I knew my performance didn't rate that much praise. He was just grateful to see me doing a half decent job, grateful his performance as Othello wouldn't be completely spoiled. But finally, at last, I had begun to understand Desdemona. Her behavior made some sense to me.

I, of course, had my principles and I was wiser than poor Desdemona who let her heart prevail when she should have listened to her head. And so, rather pleased that my Desdemona would at least be passable, I headed toward my dressing room.

As usual, the passageway was dark and only dimly lit. I hurried down it, tired, and just wanting to get home.

I pushed open the door to Nell's dressing room, now mine, and, not bothering to light the lamp, started across the darkening room past the changing screen to where my cloak hung. But a prickling on the back of my neck made me pause. Maybe I should have lit a light. After all, two women had been murdered in this room. If only I hadn't insisted on moving my things, if only I were back in my old —

A floorboard creaked behind me making the hair on the back of my neck stand up. Someone was in the room with me! I started to turn.

But I was too late. From behind me someone clapped a hand over my mouth. Probably a dirty hand, I thought with complete illogic as I tried unsuccessfully to bite it.

The man's other arm gripped me about the waist. I hadn't actually seen him, but I felt it was a man. I could smell tobacco smoke on him and another undefined smell that made my stomach queasy.

Then the hand that covered my mouth slid down around my throat and the one that held my waist moved up to join it. The image of Betty's purple blotchy face rose in my mind and I clawed at the hands, trying to pull them away, trying to get air, but he was too strong.

Inexorably he tightened his fingers. My hands beat the air frantically. Darkness swirled in my brain threatening to smother me. I had only seconds left. Was I going to die, meekly, like that milksop Desdemona?

Mama's pin! Where was Mama's pin? My seeking fingers found it. I pulled it free and jabbed backward, frantically, with all my waning strength.

The man let out a yowl. I jabbed again through the darkness that was closing in and his hands fell away. I slipped to the floor, blessed air rushing in to fill my lungs.

I had gathered just enough air to manage a scream when the door burst open and Archie rushed in. But the attacker was already gone, scrambling out the half-opened window.

His face pale, Archie hurried to my side. "Kate! Kate, love, are you all right?"

"I — I think so." Now that the danger was past I was trembling all over.

"My God, Kate!" Archie put an arm around me and helped me to my feet. "What happened?"

"A man — I think he was waiting for me. He —" My trembling fingers went to my aching throat. "Archie, he tried to strangle me."

"Good God!" Archie cried. "I knew it! I knew I shouldn't leave you alone in this abominable room. That's why I didn't go home. I stayed and watched rehearsals from the back of the theater. I was coming to tell you so and offer you a ride home when I heard the commotion."

"I stabbed him," I said, looking down at the pin I still clutched. "He went out the window. I think it was already open."

Archie helped me to the bench, then took a candle and crossed the room to examine the windowsill. "Looks like he jimmied it open! He must have come in that way. But why?"

Wearily, I shook my head. "I don't know."

"Well," he said soberly, "this settles it. I'm not leaving you alone in this room again."

"But Archie," I protested, though only halfheartedly, "you can't be here all the time."

Archie's face took on his stubborn look. "Yes, I can," he declared. "You're not going to be left in danger again."

"Yes, Archie," I said meekly, too shaken to argue with him any more. I got to my feet, certain that bruises were already starting to appear on my neck. "Please, I want to go home."

"But Constable Kennedy —"

"Oh, Archie, I can't deal with that awful man tonight. Moreover you know it won't do the least bit of good. He won't believe this is connected to the murders."

Archie shuddered, his eyes growing dark. "But you do?"

"Yes, I'm afraid I do."

CHAPTER THIRTEEN

The next morning I woke early and lay staring up at my bed curtains. I was still shaky and my throat hurt, but worst of all was the knowledge that someone had tried to kill me. Before that I'd sometimes felt bad for suspecting that people I knew might be murderers. Now I couldn't worry about that. Someone wanted to kill *me.*

A shiver sped over me as I recalled Papa crying out in tragic tones, "Death comes for Desdemona!" But Papa was always dramatic. It was just coincidence that I was playing Desdemona. Surely that had nothing to do with the attack on me.

But could I have been attacked because I was there, in Nell's dressing room? Betty had been strangled there, then Nell, and now someone had tried — Again I could feel the man's hands around my throat, choking the life out of me. My heart pounded and my mouth went dry. If it hadn't been for Mama's pin. . . .

I tried to put the awful memory out of my mind and think instead of who it might have been. Peter? But it hadn't seemed like him.

Foxcroft? He wouldn't dirty his aristocratic hands with murder. Besides, he would not have had such a rank smell to him.

And surely it couldn't have been Lavinia. Though she was big and strong enough to strangle someone, she was in prison.

Of course any one of them could have hired someone else to do it. As Archie had pointed out, London had plenty of ruffians willing to do anything for the proper price.

So, I didn't know *who* but I thought I knew *why.* No one had bothered me in the other dressing room, so it must have something to do with the room itself. The killer thought there was something in that room, something that might give him away. But what? The paper? I'd been over and over everything in the room. If the paper was there, how could I have missed it?

I sighed and threw back the covers. Time to get up and wash. I wrapped a silk scarf around my neck to hide the bruises. In two days I had to face the audience as Desdemona. I needed to run over lines, not waste time on this unsolvable puzzle except . . .

that this time it was my life in danger.

Archie arrived while we were finishing breakfast. I let him in and pointedly didn't invite him to sit down. "Good morning, Archie." I grabbed up my bonnet. "How kind of you. Shall we go see Mrs. Wattly this morning?"

I tried to shepherd him back out the door before he could say anything disastrous. I hadn't told my parents about the attack. Neither of them would have closed their eyes if they'd known about it and I wanted to get Archie out of there before he mentioned it.

But he remained obstinately where he was. "We can see Mrs. Wattly later. First we have to go to Bow Street and report —"

"Let's go then," I interrupted, grabbing his arm and pulling him toward the door.

But Papa looked up from his steak and kidney pie. "Report?" he repeated.

Archie turned accusing eyes on me. "You didn't tell them."

"No, I didn't. Come on, let's go."

"Kate!" Papa put down his fork. "You're not going anywhere until you explain what this is all about."

I glared at Archie. "Now see what you've done?"

"You should have done it yourself," he returned stubbornly. I wasn't sure I liked this stronger, more confident Archie.

"Kate," Papa said, fixing me with an annoyed look. "Kindly tell me what this is about so I can get back to my breakfast."

I gave in. "It wasn't much, really Papa, just that yesterday, after rehearsal, someone broke into my dressing room."

Mama's cup clanked against her saucer with a great clatter.

I sent Archie a warning glance. "But it was nothing."

"Nothing!" Archie cried, ignoring my warning. "The man tried to strangle you!"

Mama went pale and I could cheerfully have strangled Archie. Instead I hurried to her side. "It's all right, Mama. Really. When I jabbed him with your pin, he yelled and jumped out the window. Just then Archie came."

Papa was sitting there like a man stunned, his mouth hanging open. Finally he closed it enough to say, "Tried to kill you? How?"

Archie didn't wait for me to explain. "He was waiting in the darkened room and he grabbed her. Tried to choke her."

"Death," Papa said, his face gone tragic, "Death comes for Desdemona."

"But it didn't," I reminded him. "I'm

154

perfectly all right." I smiled at Mama. "Your pin saved me."

Papa shook his head. "You'll have to cancel Desdem—"

"Papa!" I couldn't believe it. In all the years I'd been part of the troupe, Papa had never once canceled a performance. "Papa, you know I can't cancel. You told Mr. Kemble I could play the part. I already tried to get him to do something else instead, but he insists on doing *Othello*."

"Don't worry, Mr. Ketterling." Archie stepped to my side, looking so noble he could have played Hamlet himself. "Your daughter will be quite safe, sir. I intend never to leave her alone in that cursed room."

For a minute Papa looked relieved, but then, as he seemed to consider the consequences of having Archie constantly with me, his face darkened again. "Kate, I —" Just then Mama leaned across the table to touch his arm and he sighed deeply. "Very well. I suppose that's for the best. But I don't like it. This whole thing is havey-cavey —"

"Precisely," Archie said, bringing out his warmest smile. "That's why I think we ought to go to Bow Street immediately and report —"

"Someone tried to kill you," Papa said, this last bit of information finally registering on him, "and you didn't tell anyone? You just came home?"

"Yes, Papa. I was very tired. Constable Kennedy, he would have kept us there for hours. Besides, he wouldn't believe —" I stopped abruptly. Papa would lecture me endlessly if he thought I was trying to uncover a murderer. And Mama. . . . "He wouldn't believe me," I finished lamely.

"Nevertheless you must go to him," Papa said. "It's a matter of principle. Things like this must be reported to the authorities." He shook his head. "Oh this wicked, wicked city!" Then he went back to his steak and kidney pie.

"Your father's right," Mama said. "You must tell the authorities what happened."

"But Mama —"

"It might help Lavinia," Archie said, obviously clutching at straws. "Since she was in prison, it couldn't have been her."

There was some logic to that, and if I didn't go, they would never give me any rest. "Oh, all right. Let's go."

Bow Street was like the rest of the London I'd seen, gray and narrow, with dirty buildings and dirtier cobblestones. The officer at the desk took us to the magistrate who was making a late breakfast and he put us in a dark little cubby-hole to wait for Constable Kennedy.

Archie made a face and offered me the cleanest chair. I made a face back at him and took it, finding it hard to sit still. I didn't expect any good to come of this "complete waste of time."

The little room was stuffy when we entered it and it grew worse with each passing minute. I took off my straw gypsy bonnet and used it to fan my hot face as more minutes dragged by.

Finally, in exasperation I turned, unfairly I suppose, on Archie. "I told you it would be like this! I can't afford to waste all this time. I have a performance to give tomorrow. I need to be at the theater."

"I know that," Archie said with that stubborn set to his chin. "But you can't give a performance if you're dead."

Did he have to be so blunt about it? I could still feel those fingers around my throat. "Don't be so dramatic, Archie. You said you aren't going to leave me alone. No one's going to hurt me if you're there."

"I should hope not," he said soberly. "But Kate, such things can't go unreported."

"And what things might that be?" Constable Kennedy asked, appearing in the doorway. He came in and closed the door, but instead of sitting, he stood there, gazing down at us with his bulgy eyes while the room grew hotter and hotter.

"Mistress Ketterling was attacked late yesterday afternoon," Archie said. "We thought it ought to be reported."

"Yesterday, ye say?" Constable Kennedy scowled. "And ye've just now come?"

Archie gave me his "I-told-you-so" look. Since he remained silent and Constable Kennedy was looking at me, I had to be the one to answer.

"The man was gone," I said. "He got clean away. I was very tired, I just went home."

Constable Kennedy's scowl got darker and he thrust out his lower lip before he asked, "And 'ow was ye attacked?"

I shivered slightly at the memory. "He tried to choke me. He — he had both hands around my neck."

Constable Kennedy turned to Archie. "And ye 'appened along in time to —"

"No." Archie shook his head. "Kate stopped him herself."

The constable gave me a surprised look. " 'E had 'is 'ands round yer neck and ye got away?"

"I stabbed him," I said, "with this pin that

I wear." I pulled it out of the bodice of my gown and showed it to him. I had already removed the cream silk scarf and Constable Kennedy eyed the bruises before examining the pin.

He rolled his eyes. "Well, I'll be." I thought I saw the beginning of respect in his face. "Iffen that ain't somethin'." He tested the end of the pin with his thumb. "Sharp, too. Yeah, I can see as 'ow that could make a man back off." He handed back the pin. "Did ye see anythin'? Can ye describe 'im?"

"No, I'm afraid not." I fanned myself with my handkerchief. "I was close to passing out from lack of air, you know. The first thing I thought of was breathing. After that I screamed."

"Ummmm, I see." Constable Kennedy marched back and forth in the little room with his peculiar stiff-legged rooster gait. Finally he faced me once more. "Anythin' missin'?"

"No." I hadn't really checked. But I only had costumes and makeup. A thief had no use for those. "Besides, I don't think it was a thief."

Constable Kennedy's scowl deepened. "And why not?"

"I think it was in some way connected to Nell's murder — and Betty's."

Constable Kennedy glared at me. "I told ye afore, miss, if there's a connection, and I ain't sayin' there is, Bow Street will find it. Amateurs," he sent Archie a telling look, "amateurs shouldn't be mixin' in Bow Street business."

I managed to nod, but the constable looked like he knew more than he was saying and I meant to know what it was. "Constable —"

"At least," Archie interrupted, his tone soothing and reasonable. "This attack can't be laid at Lavinia Patrick's door. She was imprisoned at the time it happened — falsely it appears now."

Constable Kennedy smiled unpleasantly. "That's where yer wrong, milord. Dead wrong, we might say." And he chuckled at his own wittiness.

I stared at him. "Surely you can see that this attack on me proves Lavinia's innocence."

"Might," Constable Kennedy said, thrusting out his lower lip. "Mebbe, if we 'ad someone else who saw this fella."

Archie bristled. "Are you doubting Mistress Ketterling's word?"

Constable Kennedy's lip thrust out even further. "No, milord. But she's the only one as saw the fella. Anyway, there's another

160

reason why this don't prove the Patrick woman's innocence."

"And what is that?" I asked caustically.

"Lavinia Patrick weren't in gaol at the time ye was attacked."

Now what was he talking about? "She wasn't?"

"Nay. She was released about two o'clock."

Archie gave the constable a hard look. "But when I was here in the morning I was told she couldn't be released."

Constable Kennedy shrugged. "Can't speak to that. Jest know we was told to let her go." He smiled slyly. "Looks like now we got reason to bring 'er in agin."

"Reason?" I repeated.

"Aye, she attacked ye."

I couldn't believe such stubbornness. "That's ridiculous. I told you — the man went out the window! Lavinia could never get out that window." At least I didn't think she could.

"Mebbe, mebbe not."

I barely managed to hold my temper. "Constable Kennedy, if there's nothing more you require of me, I must get to the theater. I'm playing Desdemona tomorrow night."

"Too bad," he said, shaking his head. "You

ain't the type fer it."

Since he was right, I kept quiet. It took a lot of effort.

"Yeah, ye can go now," he said. "I'll be sendin' a man over to 'ave a look at that window." He glanced at Archie, very man to man. "I'd keep a good eye on 'er, if I was ye, milord. She's a pretty thin', though a trifle sharp in the tongue, but she don't seem to have much sense."

"That's true," Archie said with a warning look at me to hold my tongue. "But you know how it is — a certain woman — she gets to you and you just —"

The constable smiled, a real, warm, human smile. It so transformed the man that I stared at him in surprise. "Aye, milord, that I do." He lowered his voice and actually winked at Archie. "I married mine. Been together these twenty years. And 'er jest as pretty as ever."

I was so bemused by the thought of the constable as the loving husband of a pretty Mrs. Kennedy that I kept silent and allowed Archie to lead me out.

But I had plenty to say on the way to the theater. As soon as I plunked myself down in the carriage, I turned and glared at him.

"Now see what you've done? You and your
—"

Archie's face was turning pink. "Kate,
love, be reasonable."

"Reasonable?" I cried. "I don't want to be
reasonable! Now Papa's all upset. Mama
won't be able to sleep a wink. They're going
to arrest Lavinia again. And it's all your
fault! The whole stupid thing!"

For a long moment Archie remained
silent, his back stiff, his face growing red.
He took a deep breath and I braced myself,
waiting for his outburst.

"Perhaps you're right," he said quietly.
"But Kate, you know I meant it for the
best." He leaned toward me. "I'm sorry. Will
you forgive me?"

I stared at him, my anger draining. How
could I stay angry? Besides, I knew he was
right. No matter how incompetent I thought
the authorities were I did have to report the
attack.

Archie was staring at me in tense silence,
his eyes worried. I covered his gloved hand
with my own. "I'm sorry, too," I said con-
tritely. "I know you meant well. It's just —
I'm still all on edge. And having to play
Desdemona isn't helping."

Archie nodded. "I understand." He gave
me a tiny tentative smile. "Perhaps, then,

we could forgive each other?"

"Yes." I squeezed his hand. "Yes, Archie."

His cheeky grin reappeared. "Thank goodness." He sent me an amused look. "And thank goodness you managed to keep your tongue between your teeth at the end." He chuckled and patted my hand. "Poor dear, I thought you might explode all over Constable Kennedy."

I laughed. "Oh, Archie, can you imagine Constable Kennedy with a pretty wife? I never would have thought of such a thing!"

Archie put his arm around me, a freedom I allowed because we were riding in his closed carriage. Besides, I rather liked it. "Perhaps she's beautiful only to him," he said, smiling at me gently. "They say beauty lies in the eyes of the beholder."

There was that lump in my throat again and I had to swallow hard. "I've heard that, Archie."

I was so very comfortable there, with Archie's arm around me, that I stayed that way till we reached the theater. I judged that if we had much further to go, Archie would kiss me. I recognized the heated look in his eyes, and indeed, I was feeling more than a little warm myself, warmth that had nothing to do with the weather.

Just as Archie leaned toward me the carriage came to a stop outside Covent Garden. He straightened. "I'm coming in with you. You won't be out of my sight till you're safe at home with your parents again."

"Yes, Archie." I rather liked this protective attitude, though I could see that it might become tiresome eventually. Still, I hadn't forgotten those hands around my throat and I didn't want to be alone in that dressing room.

Archie opened the door, stepped out, and turned to help me down, but before we could move Brinson came hurrying up.

"Milord," Brinson panted. "I've been — looking all — over for you. Thought you might — be here."

"Yes, man. Take your time."

Brinson nodded and gulped in air. "Mrs. Wattly — says Willie — wants to talk."

"Very good," Archie said. "Quite right of you to think of looking for me here. When you've caught your breath, go back to Mrs. Wattly. Tell her we'll be there." He looked to me. "After rehearsal?"

"Yes."

Brinson hurried off and I pressed Archie's arm. "Oh, Archie, what do you suppose Willie wants to tell us?"

"Can't say." Archie consulted his pocket

watch. "Better get inside now. You don't want to be late."

CHAPTER FOURTEEN

True to his word, Archie stuck close to me. He went to my dressing room with me, and to the stage, and back to my dressing room. He never left me alone for an instant.

And as soon as rehearsal was over we set off for Fleet Street. The sun was shining, and though they didn't smell any better, the crowded streets looked almost pleasant, but maybe that was because I was excited about what Willie might tell us. Maybe at last we'd be able to find Betty's killer . . . and Nell's, of course.

Inside the building the steps were as dark and filthy as ever, and the contrast from the sunshine made it even harder to see. The smell seemed worse, too.

Evidently Willie was listening for our tread on the stairs because before we got entirely to the top he opened the door a crack, and we used the dim light from it as a beacon. When Willie saw who was coming, he opened the door wider and hurried us in.

Inside the room I had to swallow hastily. The place smelled, a stale peculiar odor that turned my stomach. I looked at Archie, but he didn't seem to notice anything unusual.

Mrs. Wattly was sitting on a low stool by the dirty window, a costume over her lap, her needle moving busily. No doubt she'd chosen the spot so she could take advantage of the daylight while she stitched. She paused and looked up. "Afternoon, Miss Kate. I'm just finishin' up the Desdemona costumes. They'll all be ready on time." She frowned. "Then I'll be gettin' ta the others — on the cot there. Sorry I'm so long at it."

I smiled at her. "It's all right, Ms. Wattly. I didn't expect you to finish them all right away. There's plenty of time for the others."

Footsteps echoed on the landing and Willie glanced nervously at the door. His big face was so pale that he looked frightened.

Archie approached him. "I appreciate your seeing us, Willie. What do you have to tell us?"

Willie motioned us to a battered little table with three unmatched chairs around it. I was glad to see the room was getting a little homier. Even a tiny fire burned on the hearth.

"Sit down," Willie said. "I ain't got much ta tell."

The three of us took seats around the table and Mrs. Wattly went on stitching by the window.

"All right, Willie," Archie said, "go ahead."

Willie's big face paled even more. "Don't tell nobody what I tell you. It ain't safe. Specially not Bow Street."

I nodded. He didn't need to worry about that. I wouldn't be making any more trips to Bow Street if I could help it. And I certainly wouldn't trust Constable Kennedy with any important information.

Willie looked at me, his face twisting. "You got ta be careful, Miss Kate. You could be hurt just like my poor Betty."

I shivered slightly — I wasn't likely to forget my near brush with death — and pulled in a deep breath. What was that smell? Vaguely familiar, it nagged at my nose and my stomach, but I couldn't place it.

"But why, Willie?" Archie asked. "What did Betty know?"

Willie hung his head sheepishly. "I dunno fer sure. We argued 'bout it but she said as it was too dangerous. I jest know she was that worried. . . . Somethin' 'bout Mistress Standish."

Archie cast me a look. "Did Betty mention a piece of paper?"

Willie screwed his forehead into a frown. "Well, she was upset 'bout not being able ta find some piece of paper, whatever it was. But I was worried 'bout other things then, and mebbe I weren't listening so good."

"What other things?" I asked.

"Well, the Robson 'n Fisher fight. A big match, it was, Robson was the favorite. But he lost. And there's some as says the fight weren't fair, that Robson took a cross. That's how Bob and me figure it too."

I gave Archie my "I-told-you-so" look and sat up straighter. "Do some say who arranged the cross?"

Willie looked down at his big hands. "Ain't safe ta know things like that, Miss Kate, nor ta talk about 'em. Could of been anyone with blunt ta pay. Robson's the kind as would sell his own mother. But 'twas Lord Racton won the most ready, won real big so's I heard."

"And Lord Foxcroft?" I asked. "Did he wager?"

"Aye. I 'spose so." Willie paused. "His lordship comes betimes to the Cock and Bull. I know he likes the Fancy. I seen him at matches. But he ain't gonna mind no losses. A man like him." He frowned. "Now that Peter Rutherford, he bets big."

Peter betting? Could he be the killer?

Willie frowned. "But don't see how he could fix no fights. Fixing takes the ready, lots of it."

I digested this.

Willie cleared his throat. "There's more."

"Go on," Archie said.

"Couple days after the fight Lord Racton gets killed. Knifed by some footpads. Then Fisher comes up dead in an alley." Willie frowned. "It seems real strange, the two o' 'em getting kilt so close like." He rubbed his big hands together. "If the fight was fixed, no one knows who done it."

Willie was silent for some minutes. Then he sighed. "Betty were feared fer me. She didn't want me ta do no bad things. I ain't never throwed no fights." He wiped at his eyes with the back of his hand. "That's all I know, God's truth."

"That's a lot," Archie said, clapping him encouragingly on the shoulder. Archie was being kind. Without that paper, I couldn't see that this was any help at all.

Willie shook his shaggy head. "Don't see as how any o' that can help, but I told what I know. My poor Betty." He lowered his head into his hands hiding his sorrowful face.

After a few minutes the odor began to get

to me again. I felt like I couldn't breathe. I got to my feet. "I've got to get back to the theater. Thank you again, Willie."

He raised his head. "You was a friend ta my Betty. I ain't fergettin' that."

Mrs. Wattly, who was still industriously stitching, looked up. "If you'd o' come an hour or so later I'd of had the hemmin' o' these Desdemona costumes done."

"That's all right," Archie said. "Brinson'll come round later and pick them up."

We made our goodbyes and went down the dismal stairs to Archie's carriage. "It's just not fair," I said, settling into the seat. "I thought Willie really knew something. But none of this makes sense. Peter can't afford to set up a cross. And Foxcroft didn't win heavily."

"Not that he needed to," Archie said. "He's one of the wealthiest men in England."

I nodded. Foxcroft wouldn't be afraid to wager. He was the sort who'd risk a lot and always expect to win. I couldn't see what this had to do with Nell or Betty's death.

"Well," Archie said, "we're no closer to the truth than we were before." And he leaned back and looked out the window.

"I guess not." I leaned back, too, and

pulled in a big breath of air. Then I straightened. My God! That's where I'd smelled that sickening smell before!

"Archie," I stammered, "do you suppose . . ." I hated to put it into words, but I had to — that smell was still fresh in my nostrils. "Archie, do you suppose Willie could have killed Betty?"

Archie swiveled and stared at me in appalled silence, his mouth agape. Finally he said, "Willie? My God, Kate, have you lost your mind? The man loved her. Why would you think a thing like that?"

"Sometimes people kill those they love, don't they? And —"

"Not Willie." Archie's voice was vehement. "Besides, if he did it, why would he offer to talk to us?"

How was I to know that? "To throw us off, maybe, or to find out what we know."

Archie ran a hand through his hair, leaving it wilder than usual. "Did you ever see Willie at the theater?"

"I'm not sure. I think so, down in the pit. People come and go all the time, you know, and Betty could have told him how to reach the dressing room when Nell was on stage."

Archie's face was growing redder. It almost seemed that in suspecting Willie I'd insulted Archie.

He glared at me. "I don't believe it. Why, I'd sooner accuse my own mother. Really, Kate, you can't just go round accusing people of murder! As you've said yourself many times, you've got to have a reason."

"But I do!"

Archie looked exasperated. "Well, what is it? Whatever gave you this ridiculous idea?"

I ignored the insult. "The smell."

Archie's eyebrows went up. "What smell?"

"The smell in Mrs. Wattly's room. It's the same smell I noticed on the man who attacked me. I don't know what it is but I remember it. That's what makes me think maybe it was Willie."

Archie stared at me for the longest moment then to my amazement burst into laughter.

I tried to be patient but I was getting highly irritated. He laughed so long that finally I lost patience entirely. "Archie!" I jabbed him in the ribs with my elbow. "Stop it. There's nothing funny about this!"

Archie took out a clean white handkerchief and wiped his eyes. "Oh, Kate, Kate, darling Kate. I know that. What you smelled was cabbage and tobacco smoke. On any given night you can smell that odor in half the city's taverns and homes. Obviously Mrs. Wattly and Willie ate cabbage soup and

Willie smoked a pipe after."

"Cabbage soup?" I thought about the matter for some minutes, feeling foolish. Finally I said sheepishly, "I think you're right. I've smelled cabbage soup, of course. But since Papa doesn't smoke a pipe, I'd never smelled the two mixed together. Except when that man . . ."

Archie reached out to cover my hand with his. "Ah, Kate, my dear, you make my life such a joy. Surely you can't think poor Willie is pretending such sorrow."

"He might be," I insisted though I didn't believe it.

Archie snorted. "Well if Wild Man Willie isn't telling the truth, I'll — I'll —" Evidently he couldn't find anything sufficiently impressive to finish with. "I just can't believe he's a killer."

CHAPTER FIFTEEN

The next day Archie again accompanied me everywhere I went, and I appreciated it, too. His cheerful chatter was just what I needed to settle my nerves, or at least, since nothing could really settle them, to help me stay as calm as I could.

I was really nervous about playing Desdemona. My art was important to me and I didn't like the idea of making a fool of myself in front of the audience. I was doing better, but even with my newly acquired insight, I wasn't going to come close to the great Siddons in that role. The critic at the *Times* would no doubt have some acerbic things to say about my performance.

But I had to go on. There was no way to get around Mr. Kemble and I knew better than to try.

When I had my costume and makeup on, Archie escorted me to the greenroom to wait for my call.

"I'll stay here with you," he offered, "instead of going out to my box."

I was tempted to let him. Not because I was worried about being attacked, but because I didn't want Archie to witness my poor Desdemona. But that was hardly fair. "No, Archie," I said, flashing a confident smile (sometimes I really am quite an actress). "You go ahead. Go out so you can see the play."

He looked around a little nervously as though afraid to leave me. "Well, you have to change later."

"But Brinson will be waiting, just as we planned. Archie, I'm quite safe with the others here. And I promise you I won't go anywhere without Brinson. You go out to your box. I need you to see the play so afterward you can tell me how I can improve my part."

Archie grinned, a tender look coming onto his face. "Dearest Kate, don't you know that in my eyes you're already perfect?"

I laughed. "Wait till you've seen me play Desdemona. That'll change your mind."

"Never." Archie gave me a quick kiss and hurried out to his box. I settled myself on one of the red velvet chairs and tried to believe I was going to do well, but I couldn't keep my mind on the play. All I could think about was the murderer. He knew he'd failed to kill me. Would he try again?

I shivered. Of course he would. But I couldn't go on living in fear all the time. I had to figure out who the murderer was and what he was after. Was it that paper?

I thought and thought about that paper. If there was a paper and I made the killer think I had it . . .

"Miss Ketterling?"

I looked up to find Brinson standing in front of me, his face flushed and eager. "Yes?"

He glanced around the greenroom in awe and took a deep breath. "I'm here, miss, just like his lordship said."

I nodded. Sometimes I suspected Brinson should have gone into the theater. He obviously loved being backstage and he invested everything with drama.

"I won't leave you."

"Thank you."

He cleared his throat. "Mrs. Wattly asked me to bring you this."

Several people looked our way in curiosity. I took the piece of paper. Could it be? I stared down at it, then swallowed an exclamation of disgust — a list of supplies, a stupid list of. . . .

I got to my feet. "Brinson," I said. "Come

with me."

When the performance was over at last, I made my way, Brinson right behind me, back to my dressing room. He checked out the room then waited with his back to me while I hurried behind the screen and changed out of my last act nightdress and into my newest gown.

I was fairly pleased with my performance. There had even been moments, brief moments, when I felt I'd actually been better than adequate. I was eager to see Archie, to find out what he thought about it — if not from his words at least from his expression.

The greenroom was packed, and Archie was clear across it, by the red velvet drapes, cornered by the young actress who'd managed to get through the part of Emilia with only a few prompts, and was now no doubt busy regaling him with the unwanted details.

Then I saw Lavinia, her face wreathed in smiles. I hurried to her, clasping her hands in mine. "Lavinia! It's good to have you back. Thank goodness Constable Kennedy has finally gotten some sense."

She smiled back. "I hope so. Sorry I missed your performance tonight. I just got here." She gestured. "But don't let me keep you. Your Archie's been looking for you."

"Thanks, see you later."

I started out again, but then Peter reached out to put a hand on my arm. "Great job, Kate," he said with a friendly smile. "I didn't think you had it in you."

I smiled back. "Neither did I. You weren't so bad yourself." Actually he'd done little more than a passable job in his minor role, but I was feeling expansive.

Before I could say more, Brinson came rushing into the room crying, "Miss Ketterling!" He looked around furtively, then hurried to my side.

"Yes, Brinson?"

He looked around again, even more furtively. "Betty's mother," he whispered in a tone that could be heard half across the room. "She sent you this," and he passed me a folded piece of paper.

I took the paper and tried to silence him. "Thank you. You may go."

He stammered on. "She can't read, but she thought —"

"That's all, Brinson." I waved him out. Then I stuck the folded paper down inside my bodice.

Peter's smile faded and he moved away to talk to Lavinia. Was that fear I'd seen in his eyes?

"Kate, dear Kate," Foxcroft purred behind

me. The hair on the back of my neck prickled. His lips so close to my ear sent shivers up my spine.

I turned to face him. "Good evening, milord."

"You've outdone yourself tonight," he said, leaning so close to me that I could smell the starch in his neck cloth. "I knew you were among the best in breeches parts," he breathed. "I never expected you to be equally adept at tragedy. Why, when she hears of this, Mrs. Siddons will be green with envy."

"Thank you, milord." Why was he telling me my performance had rivaled that of the greatest tragedienne of our time? What was his motive, his *why?*

He leaned closer and his eyes grew warmer. When I lowered my gaze in what I hoped was a demure manner, he slid his hand up my bare arm, letting it rest familiarly on my elbow. A shiver sped up my spine. "I'm having a little party tonight," he said softly. "An intimate gathering of friends. And I should like it very much if you'd come along with me — to meet those friends." His fingers were warm, his words persuasive. And his eyes said that he wanted me. Me.

I hesitated, my heart pounding.

"You will come, won't you?" Foxcroft urged.

"I — How kind of you to ask me."

"Kate! There you are." Archie had worked his way through the crowd and stood beside me, thinking to rescue me, no doubt, from Foxcroft's unwanted attentions. "Kate, love, I —"

And in that moment I made up my mind. This was my chance. "*Will* you let me be?" I cried, turning half the heads in the room with my screeching. "The answer is no! No! No! No! Now go away and leave me alone!"

While Archie stood stunned, his eyes full of reproach, I took Lord Foxcroft's arm and leaned against him. "I'm ready, milord. Shall we go?"

Foxcroft smiled and led me out, past the envious young actresses and staring actors, past a white-faced Peter and a Lavinia who looked stricken. I glanced around but Brinson was nowhere to be seen.

CHAPTER SIXTEEN

Foxcroft's mansion sat in Grosvenor Square, a great huge place, every window ablaze with light, a fitting house for such a grand lord.

As the butler greeted us, I heard voices and laughter coming from down the hall, but when I started that way, Foxcroft smiled and shook his head. "I dragged you away from the theater so quickly, my dear, you had no chance to freshen up. Come with me and we'll remedy that."

He turned and led me in the opposite direction. The hall of that grand mansion, wide as a room, had niches on each side where life-sized statues stood, and, in between, gilded paintings hung above velvet covered chairs, and polished tables held great vases of fresh flowers.

All the footmen remained on duty in the foyer. Not one offered to follow us, and the sounds from the other side of the house slowly faded.

Some way down the hall Foxcroft pushed open a paneled mahogany door and motioned me to enter. I stepped in, gazing around in wonderment. I'd never been in such a richly appointed room. Everything in it, from the fine lace curtains on the French doors to the heavily carved green velvet chairs and settees to the fine glass lamp on the polished table, everything bespoke money.

A sharp click brought my thoughts back to the man who was lord of all this. I turned to see him tucking the key to the hall door into his waistcoat pocket. "So we won't be disturbed," he said smoothly.

I swallowed nervously. "If you'll just show me to a mirror," I said, "I'll fix my hair and we can meet your friends."

"I think not." A strange smile crossed his face. "I'm afraid this party is going to be more intimate than you expected. Only you and I, in fact."

He took a step toward me and I backed a step away, slowly. "Really, milord, you invited me to a party, not to a private —"

"What a fool you are," he said, his strange eyes burning into me. "I don't see how Cripps could have failed."

"Cripps?" I echoed.

"Yes, Cripps. I hired him to get rid of that eavesdropping maid. She overheard Nell blackmailing me." His smile made my flesh crawl. How could I ever have been attracted to this man?

"I took care of Nell myself. Later I sent Cripps back for you but he botched the job."

I stared at him with my best expression of shock. "How could you — how could you kill a woman you'd —?"

He laughed again, an essentially evil sound. "Come now, surely you don't expect me to have tender feelings for someone who was blackmailing me. She wouldn't tell Rutherford —"

"Peter?" Now I was genuinely shocked. "What has Peter to do with this?"

"I hired him to pry the whereabouts of a certain piece of paper from Nell." While he talked, he took the key from his pocket, tossing it from hand to hand, the cat playing with the mouse. "But the idiot fell in love with her. Imagine — in love with that . . ." He shook his head ruefully.

"What piece of paper?" I asked, deliberately making my voice weak, though it didn't take much effort.

Foxcroft tossed the key and caught it again, his gaze going to my bosom. "Maybe the one you have tucked in your bodice."

"Oh, that's nothing," I stammered.

He put out a hand and his eyes went even colder. "Give it to me, or I'll take it."

I gave it to him without hesitation. I didn't want his hands on me. "It's only a list."

He opened it. "So it is — appears to be a list of supplies."

"From my seamstress. The footman wrote it out for her."

He laughed, a strange crazy note in the sound. "So I didn't need to bring you here tonight. But now that I have. . . ." He laughed again. "You see, I've been looking for a piece of paper, a piece of paper that tells the unfortunate details of my involvement in the Robson-Fisher fight. Peter couldn't find it." He laughed again. "She hid it so well no one found it."

He shook a finger at me playfully. "You shouldn't have gone poking about as you did, my dear. True, I didn't recognize you that night at the Cock and Bull, at least not till I saw you in your breeches playing Sir Harry Wildair. Then I realized it was you I'd seen. I also heard a description of the lad who was asking about crosses at the Robson-Thicket match."

My mind raced. "It's true I was snooping," I said, "but I didn't learn anything. You were much too clever." I swallowed hard and went on. "When I asked around about the Robson-Fisher fight, no one knew who fixed it."

"Racton did it," he said darkly, cursing.

"I wagered and I lost," he went on. "Lost heavily." He took a step toward me and I edged backward a little. "Then I found it was a cross, a cross Racton set up."

"So you had him killed so you wouldn't have to pay."

He stared at me in surprise. "Of course not. It was a debt of honor. I paid it."

"Then why —"

"He laughed at me, crowed over what he'd done, I stopped his mouth. No one laughs at me." His face at that moment was truly evil. "When that simpleton Fisher drank too much and started babbling, he had to be silenced too."

Foxcroft looked deep into my eyes, and I imagined it was like looking at one of those snakes that hypnotize their prey before they strike. "Now I'm going to kill you."

"But — but —" I stammered. "Why did you tell Nell about these murders?"

"I didn't tell her," he said. "She listened at the door of my study one night. She wrote it all down and hid it. She was too greedy. She wanted too much." He smiled and turned my blood cold. Then he made a big show of dropping the key in his pocket again. "I'd never killed anyone before Nell." He looked down at his hands, almost as though he'd never seen them before, then back up at me. He shrugged. "It's just something that has to be done."

"I —"

"Don't beg now," he mocked. "It was really ill-advised of you, a second-rate actress, to match wits with me."

I bit my tongue. Now was not the time to defend my theatrical honor, nor my intelligence.

I eased backward another step, never taking my gaze from his face. The French doors were somewhere to my right. I didn't dare to glance that way, but a lamp stood on a table to this side, and I could see the halo of light it spread on the Persian rug. If I could get to that lamp, if I could throw it . . .

"Please, milord." I put my hand to my heart over Mama's pin. "Please, I won't tell anyone. Even if I did, no one would believe me."

He laughed mockingly. "You're probably right. But I'm going to make an end of this — and of you. This one little thing and it'll all be over."

"Please, milord —" I withdrew my hand

from my heart, the pin hidden in it, and kept that hand in the fold of my skirt. "I've hardly lived yet," I pleaded, acutely aware that I was speaking the truth. "I don't want to die. And — and how can you explain me being dead — here?"

"Quite easily," he said. "Lavinia Patrick has been released." He shrugged. "You won't be found here. They'll come across your poor body in an alley near her rooms. And I shall say that you left here with Lavinia, foolish trusting girl that you are. Who's to doubt my word?"

Archie would doubt it, but I didn't say that. Foxcroft's power seemed to have made him mad. He actually believed he could do anything he wanted to do. But no man was above the law — not indefinitely.

By that time he had me backed against the outside wall. The lamp was only a few feet away but he stood between it and me. Towering over me as he did, his physical presence was almost overpowering.

He smiled, a smile almost as frightening as his words, and leaned forward to finger a lock of my hair. "It's a pity you had to ruin things," he purred. "You're a pretty little piece. Who knows, you might have taken Nell's place, for a little while anyway."

I lowered my gaze, just a little. "I'm sorry,

too, milord," I said humbly. Anything to postpone his hands around my neck. I remembered those other hands, choking the life out of me, and I tried not to panic. "I've — I've never been kissed by a man like you."

He actually chuckled. "I suppose I can remedy that. I'd hate to send you to your grave having only been kissed by that milksop Barrington."

I kept my expression yielding, but I remembered Archie's kisses longingly. Would I ever know them again?

Then Foxcroft reached out and pulled me into his arms. I didn't scream. I didn't shiver. I didn't resist at all. In fact, I raised my arms to put them around his neck. His lips touched mine —

And I stabbed him with my pin right above his cravat. When he bellowed in pain and grabbed for his neck, I slipped under his flailing arms, snatched up the lamp, and hurled it through the window of the French doors.

I was about to throw myself after it — I'd rather take my chances with broken glass than with Foxcroft's hands — when Archie came charging in through them, and, pounding right after him, Willie and Bruising Bob.

Archie jumped at Foxcroft and began

pummeling him. Foxcroft fought back, of course, and they careened around the room, crashing against the furniture. They bounced into a delicate table, and a crystal water pitcher flew off, water puddling on the polished wood floor as they grappled toward the windows.

Then they came back across the room, throwing blows at each other. Foxcroft stepped backward and slipped in the water. He went down, hitting his head on the floor. Archie was on in him a second, straddling him, but Foxcroft didn't move. The fall must have knocked him out. Archie raised his fists, his face white with anger.

"Archie!" I yelled, pulling at him. "Stop! You'll kill him!"

"Aye, milord." Willie added his voice to mine. "Stop now. 'E'll hang, 'e will." His face worked furiously. "Though I'd like ta have the finishin' o' 'im meself."

The noise had brought Foxcroft's servants to pound on the locked door. Willie and Bob exchanged looks and moved between the door and Archie. When the door burst open and the servants came crashing in, Willie and Bob tangled with them, fists and shouts all around. Archie hit Foxcroft again because he was stirring, and I stood near them, clutching my pin and not knowing what to do.

I was looking around for something else to use as a weapon when Constable Kennedy pushed through the French doors, followed by his men and Peter! "Enough," the constable bellowed. Willie and Bob and the servants all froze, standing in awed silence. "That's better now," the constable said. He turned to Archie. "We'll jest be taking 'im now, milord."

Willie and Bob pulled Archie off of Foxcroft. The servants stood staring as the police hauled their master to his feet like a common criminal.

The constable said, "That'll be enough now. You'd best be gettin' to yer business. I'll take care of 'is lordship."

"You'll pay for this," Foxcroft snarled, baring his teeth. How could I ever have been attracted to the man? "You'll all pay!" And cursing me, Peter, Nell, the sport of boxing, and life in general, he was taken away. At a gesture from Constable Kennedy the servants left the room, too.

"You've no need to worry, miss," Constable Kennedy said to me softly. " 'E won't be killin' anyone again. Nor 'irin' it done neither."

"You know?"

His chest swelled out a little. "Aye. Mr.

192

Rutherford there," he motioned to Peter, "he told us the whole story. We had our suspicions afore that but nothin' we could prove." He frowned. "With someone like Lord Foxcroft, well — we 'ad to be sure."

He patted my arm. "Ye just come along to the station in the morning, miss. We'll be needing the two of ye to make a report. But there's no rush." He gave me a kindly smile. "Ye'd best be lookin' to yer friend." And he went out with the rest of his men.

Archie's knuckles were bleeding and his chest was heaving, but otherwise he seemed all right. He moved toward me. "Oh, Archie, I —"

"Kate," Peter said, coming up to us. "I'm so sorry about all this."

I stared at him, thinking of Betty's useless killing, then I told him, "You brought the Runners to help me, and you told them what you knew."

Peter looked sheepish. "Well, that wasn't all my idea."

"It wasn't?"

"It was Lavinia's." Peter looked toward the broken French doors where I saw her hesitating. When I motioned, she came to join us.

"We saw you go with Foxcroft," she said, "and then when Bob and Willie came —"

"Bob? Lavinia, Bruising Bob is your fellow?"

Lavinia smiled. "Yes, I thought you knew. I was just so worried to see you with Foxcroft. Then Peter told me what he suspected. We decided he should go to Bow Street for help and we'd come here, but Archie got here first."

Peter nodded. "I tried before — to warn you about Foxcroft." He frowned. "But I didn't dare. He paid me, you see, to make love to Nell so I could find out where some paper was. But she wouldn't tell me." He swallowed hard. "I really did love her. I didn't know he was going to kill her." He blinked. "Afterwards I suspected him but I couldn't prove it. When I saw you with him tonight — and Lavinia said you might . . ." He shuddered. "So I went for the Runners."

"That was very brave of you, Peter. Thank you." I gave him a big hug.

He hugged me back and then with a look at Archie stepped away. "Don't you worry now," he said. "The magistrate won't let him go free. I'm going right down there and repeat what I told the constable."

"And we're going with him," Lavinia said. "Willie and Bob mean to tell everything they know about the fight that was fixed."

Archie slipped an arm around my waist

and turned to the others. "Thank you. Thank you all."

" 'Tis nothing," Willie said, looking sheepish.

Lavinia smiled and motioned him and Bob out, leaving Archie and me alone.

Archie turned to me, his face woebegone. "Ah, Kate, my Kate, how could you do this to me? For a minute there in the greenroom I thought you were really driving me away."

"Oh, Archie, you should know I wouldn't do that. I knew Brinson would explain it to you. Didn't he play his part well? You must tell him so."

"Yes, yes." Archie shook his head. "Still, you took an awful chance going away with Foxcroft like that. What if Brinson had missed me? What if Foxcroft sent someone to stop him? What if I hadn't come after you?"

I shuddered but managed a smile. "I knew you'd follow." I pulled in a deep breath. "But for a while there I wasn't sure you'd get here in time."

Archie pulled me into his arms, holding me close. "I know you wanted to find Betty's murderer, but to come to the man's house when you knew he was the one responsible!"

I pulled back enough to see his face. "But

Archie, that's just it. I didn't know. I was almost sure, though, because he complimented me on my Desdemona."

Archie nodded. "You did a fine job."

"No, Archie. I mean he really complimented me. He said I rivaled Mrs. Siddons."

Archie's mouth fell open and he stared at me. Finally he said, "You — Mrs. Sid—"

"Yes, Mrs. Siddons. I didn't see how he could possibly believe such a thing. That's what made me suspect him. But I knew that without proof Constable Kennedy would never believe me. No one would. That's why I had Brinson give me the paper in front of all three of them, in case I suspected the wrong one."

Archie sighed. "I suppose you did right, but my God, Kate! I died a thousand deaths on the way here just thinking about it, or imagined *you* dying, which was even worse."

"I'm sorry, Archie, truly." I moved a little closer to him. "But I didn't know what else to do. I felt that missing paper was important. Then Brinson came with a list from Mrs. Wattly and I thought if the murderer believed it was . . . so I told Brinson what to do. Then I had to come along with Foxcroft to prove he was the guilty one."

"Well, you've done that," Archie said, giving me his slightly exasperated look. "You've solved the murders. You've cleared Lavinia and Peter. And now Mrs. Wattly will know Betty's killer has been brought to justice."

He held me off and gazed soberly down into my eyes. "I want you to promise me you'll never get involved in something as dangerous as this again."

Instead I chuckled. "Why, Archie, do you think I want to chase after murderers?" I sighed. "My, but I'm tired. Will you take me home now?"

He looked at my hand where I was still clutching Mama's pin, and smiled slightly. "I have my closed carriage. Have you any objection to that?"

"No," I said, sliding the pin back into my bodice. "None at all."

ABOUT THE AUTHOR

Nina Coombs Pykare has published 47 novels and novellas in the romance, inspirational, historical, contemporary, Regency, gothic, and mystery fields, but the Regency period is her favorite. She especially likes Regency theater, so an actress/sleuth was a natural.

She has published under the pen names of Ann Coombs, Nora Powers, Regina Towers, Nan Pemberton, and Nina Porter, as well as Nina Coombs, Nina Pykare, and Nina Coombs Pykare.

Nina started college at 32 after having five children, earned a Ph.D. in 18th century English literature when she was 42, and published her first novel at 46.

She has sold close to 300 short stories and has been teaching the novel writing workshop for *Writer's Digest* since its inception in 1988 and sometimes speaks at conferences and teaches local classes. She is a member of the Beau Monde Regency sub-chapter of the RWA, the RWA, and Sisters in Crime.

We hope you have enjoyed this Large Print book. Other Thorndike, Wheeler, and Chivers Press Large Print books are available at your library or directly from the publishers.

For information about current and upcoming titles, please call or write, without obligation, to:

Publisher
Thorndike Press
295 Kennedy Memorial Drive
Waterville, ME 04901
Tel. (800) 223-1244

or visit our Web site at:

www.gale.com/thorndike
www.gale.com/wheeler

OR

Chivers Large Print
published by BBC Audiobooks Ltd
St James House, The Square
Lower Bristol Road
Bath BA2 3SB
England
Tel. +44(0) 800 136919
email: bbcaudiobooks@bbc.co.uk
www.bbcaudiobooks.co.uk

All our Large Print titles are designed for easy reading, and all our books are made to last.

Imperal